MUSCLESEX

MUSCLESEX

A collection of erotic stories

Greg Nero

Leyland Publications
San Francisco

First edition 1995
Front cover photo copyright © 1995 by Terry Studio
Cover design by Rupert Kinnard
ISBN 0-943595-59-2

ACKNOWLEDGMENTS:
"Big Mac" first appeared in *Drummer*, #38; "Educating Ricky" first appeared in *Torso*, May 1989; "Class of '75" first appeared in *Advocate Men*, June 1985; "The Muscle Shoppe" first appeared in *Honcho Overload*, June 1994; "Mr. Collegiate" first appeared in *Numbers*, May & June 1981; "Stripped for Action" first appeared in *Drummer*, #169; "Most Muscular" first appeared in *Mandate*, September 1984; "No Pain, No Gain" first appeared in *Honcho Overload*, March 1994; "Texas Tits" first appeared in *Drummer* #121; "Strike Zone" first appeared in *Mach*, #29; "Tarzan the Tit Man" first appeared in *Mach*, #32; "Hard Times" first appeared in *Honcho Overload*, May 1994; "Tool Pusher" first appeared in *Drummer Rides Again!* and was reworked by the author in 1995.

Leyland Publications
P.O. Box 410690
San Francisco, CA 94141
Complete illustrated catalogue available for $1 ppd.

Contents

A bodybuilder likes two things, kid. He likes to fuck and he likes muscle, especially his own. Now, if he can combine the two, he's really got it made. Muscle and sex, there ain't nothing finer.

—*Mike Gates*, bodybuilder,
excerpt from "Most Muscular"

MuscleSex

MuscleSex is an anthology of Greg Nero stroke stories devoted to the celebration of awesome, jaw-dropping muscle and hot male sex. The gut-churning, mouth-watering buffed bods in *MuscleSex* range from sleek and sexy young studs barely out of their teens to older, more seasoned, hard-core bodybuilders and weightlifters who have become so massive and freaky-huge over the years that most people would think they're grotesque, over-developed monsters. But all perception is relative. One man's gross and disgusting is another man's awesome, heart-pounding object of desire. The men in these stories cater to a wide spectrum of beefy tastes and should satisfy even the most jaded muscle aficionado's lust for the ultimate in male perfection.

The sex in the stories ranges from "vanilla" and relatively mainstream (dare I say Harlequin Romance-esque) to something right out of a heavy-duty S&M scene. Big muscle is certainly the catalyst but muscle isn't the only thing being pumped, posed, flexed and worked out in *MuscleSex*. There's plenty of hard cocks doing all sorts of nasty, wonderful things. There's huge, protruding nipples getting worked over something fierce. There's beautiful bubble-butts getting fucked between sets of squats and—well, the list goes on. These guys are into meat and muscle in a big way. They love to pump iron, pump cock and pump tit—and they do it with a beginning, middle and an end, too. They've got everything a muscle fanatic could want.

The fifteen stories are divided into four groups: Nice and Easy, In the Gym, Rough and Tough, and Something a Little Different.

"Nice and Easy" groups those stories which portray hot, muscular men doing their thing outside the gym. The sex is relatively tame and more mainstream.

"In the Gym" groups those stories which actually take place in a gym (or locker/shower room). Again, the sex is more mainstream.

"Rough and Tough" groups those stories which portray steamy

bodybuilders in and out of the gym who prefer their sex with a rough—sometimes very rough—edge to it. This is S&M musclemansex at its best.

"Something a Little Different" has a story whose pivotal character, while obviously not a bodybuilder, is certainly a large, powerful man. He isn't a Mr. America but, for some, he will still be a major turn-on. It makes for a nice twist at the end.

Big Mac

DO YOU EVER CROSS your fingers and close your eyes, hoping that when you open them again some mind-blowing stud will have somehow materialized in front of you, smiling and wanting to get to know you better? I do it all the time. Nothing ever happens. Or, maybe I better say, nothing happened until last night.

There I was in a corner booth at McDonald's—of all fucking places. It was late, the overtime had been rough, and a dull throb in the back of my skull was trying to turn into World War III. Man, I felt the shits. All I wanted was some coffee in my gut before going home to crash out.

I heard a throat clear beside me and slowly opened my eyes. Goddamn, I almost got whiplash, I straightened up so fast! There, not two feet away, was the most incredible hunk of manhood I ever saw in my life!

Now, everyone has his own idea of what a "hunk" should look like, and it isn't every day you see a guy that knocks you for a loop but, I swear, *there was a hunk*!

Young, no more than twenty-one. Dark, piercing eyes. Full lips tightened into a streetpunk smirk, flashing sparkling white teeth. Lean face framed by a head of black hair with not a strand out of place.

Medium height. Hard jock body. Broad shoulders, deep chest, wasp waist, arms that looked about the size of my thighs. Must have lifted a lot of weights to fill out a t-shirt like that.

His cut-offs were slung low on the hip, cut high on the legs, and bulged at the crotch. His bare legs were covered with dark silky hair, which grew thicker and blacker the closer it got to the groin and, I swear, the leg muscles rippled when he shifted his weight from one sneakered foot to the other. You always read about things like that, but to actually see it happen . . .

And that cock of his! Long, thick, and cut—you could see it plain as day through the fabric! So close I could have reached out and touched it. Shit, it was all I could do to keep my hands to myself.

"Got a cigarette? I ain't got enough money for both food and smokes. Help me out, huh?"

The way his eyes effortlessly held mine, there was no way I could turn him down. But, man, who would have wanted to turn him down? He was someone I'd walk a mile for, if you know what I mean.

Like some nervous kid about to pee his pants I fumbled with my cigarette pack and breathed a sigh of relief when he finally had one lit. Marlboros.

"Thanks."

I just nodded and watched stupidly while he went to the counter to place his order. Those shoulders narrowed down to the tightest ass I ever saw in my life! What a fucking body! What a fucking tan! What a . . .

I froze when I realized he was watching me watching him. A sure, cocky smile creased the corners of his mouth.

I always thought of myself as confident and sophisticated, able to handle myself in any situation. Maybe even just a little jaded. But this kid had kicked the feet right from under me! There and then I wanted to sell my soul for just one night with him. Just one night.

"Mind if I sit down? Don't like eating alone."

I about creamed my pants when he said that. This had to be a dream, it was happening too fast. It was all too good.

"The name's Mac," he said, before biting into his burger.

"As in Big Mac?" I hinted, feeling some of the old ease returning.

Catching the innuendo, he smiled. "Yeah."

"And I'll bet your middle name is Whopper." Shit, talk about being obvious!

He must have liked it, though, because his head went back and he let out a laugh. "You bet it is!"

"I could eat whoppers all day," I said. Where the hell was I digging up these old cliches?

"You could, huh? How about this one?" And, without another word, Mac stood up on the table and slowly slid down his cutoffs. His big meat, free of its bindings, was hard in about ten seconds.

"What the hell are you doing?" I stuttered. "The fucking manager must be calling the cops by now!" I looked around to check and . . . couldn't believe my eyes. We were alone. There wasn't another person in the whole place. Just Mac and me.

I couldn't figure out what was going on!

Big Mac was sure the name for him, alright. I won't go into inches but, after all the years' experience I've had in locker rooms, I knew Mac ranked right up there with the biggest and best of them.

Bulbous cockhead, a thick baseball bat for a shaft, and two grapefruit-sized balls dangling low and heavy. All covered in a thick, black forest of hair. Pre-cum dribbled from his pisshole and fell sparkling onto the table like he was pouring the stuff from a bottle.

"What if someone sees you?" I warned, as I started licking his juice off the table.

"Who cares?" shrugged Mac, grinding his hips and dipping into a couple of low squats. Slipping his feet out of the cut-offs, he picked them up and swung them a couple of times over his head before letting go. They arced gently through the air and landed in a deep frier.

"Hot damn, I'm going to be sizzling and crispy tonight!"

"You're insane," I laughed.

"No more than you!"

Off came the t-shirt. Mac's pectorals bunched and writhed under the exertion of his flexing. His nipples were rock hard and stood out a mile. Every time he exhaled, washboard abdominals popped into view.

"Mac, you're fucking fantastic!" I screamed, pounding the table for more. "Turn around! Turn around!"

"Glad to oblige." Mac did a smart pirouette, landing on his knees, his hairy ass about five inches from my face.

Honest, even his ass rippled with muscle! Just as I was leaning forward to lick his bunghole, Mac spun around again, his monster weapon almost clubbing me across the head.

One hand squeezing the hell out of his left tit and the other whacking away at his dong, Mac's eyes were closed tight as he raced to the point of no return.

And I was racing with him! I hadn't even touched him and I felt ready to explode in a million pieces.

He started moaning. Low. Husky. Sweat poured off his body, drenching the table and splashing man-salt over me.

"I'm going to . . . going to blast off," groaned Mac, pumping harder and faster to keep pace with the spunk rushing up his poker. "I'm coming . . ."

"Sir."

"I'm coming . . . commmminnnnggggg. . . ."

"Sir. SIR!"

"Huh? What?" Someone was nudging my shoulder.

"You okay, sir?"

"What the hell do you mean, am I okay? What the hell's going on here? Where's Mac?"

"Mac? No one called Mac here."

"Oh."

"You must have been dreaming."

"Yeah." Tell me about it, kid.

"Sounded like a good one."

"Oh, shit. What do you mean?" I started wondering what I might have been doing while visiting the twilight zone.

"Well, you kept telling someone to shoot. But, hey, don't worry, I was the only person who heard you."

For the first time, I looked past the McDonald's uniform into the smiling face.

Shit, it was another hunk! Blond, surfer-type. Shoulders the proverbial mile wide, tan like you wouldn't believe, and the deepest blue eyes I ever saw in my life. I definitely liked what I saw.

"It was a good dream. Damn good." I smiled. Hmmm, he couldn't have been more than twenty-one. Probably working his way through college.

"I'd like to hear about it," he said, hitching up his pants to show the outline of a very, very hard cock. No underwear, I liked that. Devilish grin, too.

"I must be dreaming again," I said.

"No dream, I'm for real. I get off at midnight."

Somebody up there likes me. Two studs in one night. Far-fucking out. "I'll be here," I replied. "Oh, by the way. What's your name?"

"Ronald."

I tried not to choke on my coffee. "You're kidding. Really?"

"Really."

"Is your middle name Whopper?"

"What?"

"Never mind." Thank you, Mr. McDonald, wherever you are.

Educating Ricky

RICHARD ("Call me Ricky") Delvecchio was the most conceited, arrogant sonofabitch Neil had ever met in his life. The guy was amazing, truly amazing. He figured he had it all—youth, movie star good looks, a Mr. America body, charm, wit, intelligence, the charisma of a Greek god and the unbridled appeal that comes from sporting a basket that would stun the delegates of a porn convention. And as much as Neil tried to deny it, he had to admit Ricky was right. He really did have it all. He was undoubtedly the hottest man Neil had ever laid his eyes on.

Trouble was, there was no way Neil could act on any of his impulses. Not if he wanted to keep his reputation and his job. It was an open secret in the company he was gay but as the Advertising and PR Manager there were just some things he'd never get away with. Like going ga-ga over the new man in Sales and Marketing. Even if everyone else was doing just that. No, if he was going to cope with Ricky Delvecchio he'd have to maintain a strict hands-off policy.

Easier said than done. Especially when Ricky oozed sex appeal as easily as most people perspired. There were so many little things about Ricky that drove Neil crazy. Things like: smoldering brown eyes and a boyish grin; skintight pants that hugged the curves of his seductive, muscular ass and accentuated the thick slab of uncut cock he stuffed down his left pant leg; the way his broad shoulders and chiselled pecs filled out a shirt so that he almost looked bare chested; and the way his flat, dime-sized nipples puckered into inviting, perky little nubs every time he took his jacket off in an air-conditioned room.

And then there were the major causes of Neil's Ricky-induced heart attacks: hearing how pumped he got in a gym workout; watching the twin globes of his little bubblebutt flex every time he bent over; spotting him strutting through the office with a hard-on (had to be at least eight inches!); and perhaps most maddening of all, watching him at the next urinal while he played with his jumbo-sized meat long after he'd finished his business, knowing damn well he was doing it deliberately for Neil's benefit. Try and maintain a hands-off policy with someone doing that, griped Neil.

To make matters worse, Ricky *liked* him. Oh sure, Ricky liked everyone but, even after two months, it was always Neil Ricky came to if he had a question or needed advice or if he simply had a few minutes to kill. Which always struck Neil as somewhat peculiar because, according to the office grapevine, Ricky was a real hot-shot ladies' man, a Casanova of epic proportions. There was nothing Neil could verify but, if it was true, then why was he spending any time at all with him?

Sure, they had a few things in common—growing up in Texas, a stint in the Navy, a degree from UCLA and a love of sports—but certainly nothing binding enough to keep Ricky coming back for more. Oh well, Neil sighed, enjoy it while you can because sooner or later he's going to meet some dazzling young lady and then he won't have time to kill, much less time to shake his dick.

There was a knock at the door and Ricky stuck his head in. "Can I talk to you a second?"

He seemed shy, ill-at-ease, two qualities Neil didn't think he possessed. "I was just getting ready to pack it in for the weekend but, sure, come in and sit down." He closed the file he was working on and, as he usually did, took a quick glance at Ricky's squared shoulders, carved pecs, perky nipples and mouth-watering basket before settling back to talk. "Okay, what's wrong?"

Ricky nervously ran the palms of his hands up and down over his massive, tree-trunk thighs while he gathered his thoughts. In doing so, the muscles of his arms rippled, his pecs alternately tensed and relaxed and Neil's temperature sky-rocketed. "I need help," he said finally. "And you're the only person who can give it to me, the only person I'd feel comfortable with."

Neil looked up from the bulge at Ricky's crotch and swallowed hard. "What sort of help?"

"I'm supposed to do a marketing survey on the gay consumer. I got what I could from the library but I figure the only way to really get anywhere is to go out and do some firsthand research."

"Get some field experience, as it were," murmured Neil.

"Exactly!" brightened Ricky, flashing his twenty mega-watt smile. "And since I'm new in town and wouldn't know where to look, I figured you would be the best person to show me around. You know, kinda be my resource for the project. My teacher. How about it? Please?"

"Your teacher . . . geez, I don't know," Neil mumbled. If this was his big chance to get chummy with Ricky Delvecchio then why was he choking at the prospect? Funny how he couldn't remember this survey coming up at the last Sales and Marketing meeting.

"I don't want to bomb out," stated Ricky. He leaned close across the desk. "You gotta help me."

Neil's resolve melted as he stared into Ricky's determined brown eyes. What else could he say?

"That's fantastic! You're a pal, Neil. I'll owe you big for this one. You really saved my ass."

"Don't mention it," Neil chuckled. Anything, to save a truly great ass, he thought.

"Can we start tonight?"

"Tonight?"

At Ricky's insistence, so he wouldn't lose any more time he said, they met later that evening at a popular gay restaurant. Neil took one look at the handsome hunk waiting for him in the foyer and whatever remaining doubts he might have had about what he was doing vanished.

Ricky was a wet dream of male perfection. He was humpy in a business suit but in thread-bare blue jeans and muscle-hugging white T-shirt he was positively gut-wrenching.

"God, you're a hot man!" exclaimed Neil, unabashedly admiring the vision in front of him. "You're going to need a club to beat off the lionizing hordes tonight."

"I've got a club, remember?" smirked Ricky, giving his crotch a lascivious squeeze. Then with a wink he said, "Come on, let's eat. We got a long, fun-filled night ahead of us."

So they ate. And talked. At first, like he was supposed to, Neil told Ricky his ideas about the gay consumer and the direction Ricky might consider going in his project. But as the evening wore on and all the beer they were drinking took effect, business ended up taking a back seat to just about anything else. And by eleven o'clock, business was the last thing on their minds.

"Come on, Teach, let's go to a bar," urged Ricky. "You promised to show me around." He flashed that mega-watt smile and off they went.

If being in a gay bar was a new experience for Ricky he sure didn't show it. He took to the jam-packed, all-male environment like a duck to water. And it was a good thing he was used to being stared at because no matter where he and Neil staggered in the cavernous bar-cum-dance emporium he was openly gawked at and visually strip-searched.

"What a hoot!" he hollered, an hour and three beers later. The place was hotter than a furnace and his T-shirt was drenched in sweat and clinging to every rippling, defined muscle of his torso, making the five hundred or so guys watching him hornier than hell. Grinning like a Cheshire cat, he suddenly grabbed Neil about the waist, pulled him in tight and without further ado gave him a long, searching wet one right on the lips. The Earth, moon and half the solar system came to a screeching halt right then and there.

By the time Ricky finally let him up for air Neil was panting like a bellows. "What was *that* for?" he gasped in stunned surprise, acutely aware that their groins were still tightly mashed together and he, for one, had a raging hard-on.

"For taking me out and showing me a good time," smiled Ricky. "And because I felt like it. Come on, let's dance."

"Dance?" My god, I've unleashed a monster!"

"No, unleashing the monster comes later. Come on."

Man, could Ricky dance! His body was raw sex in motion, capable of turning a simple gyration into an indecent act. Neil would have been happy to just step back and watch the man move, he was so provocative, but except for brief stops for more beer Ricky kept them dancing right up until closing time.

In fact, Ricky kept them dancing long after closing time. He was such a smooth mover that it wasn't until they were back at Neil's place—"for one last beer"—that Neil really clued-in to what was happening.

"Aw, what the hell," Neil shrugged, "he's a big boy." He looked Ricky up and down and, stifling a hiccup, added, "A very big boy."

"I gotta pee," grinned Ricky. "Where's the bathroom?"

"I'll tell you," Neil leered, "if you let me watch."

Without missing a beat Ricky snickered, "Hell, I was hoping you'd hold it for me. Come on."

Like a couple of exuberant schoolboys horsing around during

recess, they jockeyed into position in front of the gleaming porcelain bowl (Neil's chest pressed tightly into Ricky's back) and got down to the business at hand. Or, rather, the business in Neil's hand.

"Oh, man," he intoned as he wrapped his fingers around Ricky's flaccid, uncut member. Soft, it was bigger than most hard cocks! After dreaming about it for so long, the reality of finally getting a hold of it was almost too much to bear. "Oh fuck, oh fuck, oh fuck," he kept saying.

"If you're through swearing," mused Ricky, "you might want to point my dick downwards before I give the wall a good hosing."

"Oh fuck, yeah."

The way he let loose, Ricky must have been saving up all night for this moment. He seemed to go on forever. Not that it bothered Neil at all. It gave him more time to hold Ricky against him, to run his free hand luxuriously over Ricky's muscled chest and nuzzle the back of his neck, where he could inhale the heady aroma of cologne and dried sweat and taste bitter-sweet salt. He could have stayed there happily for hours.

But Ricky's cock had other ideas. The splashing torrent had barely trickled to a stop when it slowly, ponderously came to life, growing steadily in Neil's hot hand until it reached its full, engorged length. A good eight inches long and so thick Neil couldn't get his hand all the way around it; it was fucking magnificent! It was a cock most men only fantasize about. With a mixture of awe and delight, Neil began fervently fist-pumping the monster meat. One stroke was nice and light and easy, the next firm and forceful, almost brutal.

"Oh, yeah," moaned Ricky. "That feels so-o-o-o good. So good. I think I'm going to like this part of the course."

"Think of it as the extra-curricular part."

"Hmmm. Well, I think it's about time the teacher got his apple!" Ricky turned and gave Neil a short, explosive kiss. Finding Neil's hard, well-worn nipples he playfully exhorted, "Come on, Teach, time for some one on one!"

Practically stumbling over each other in their mad, frenzied lust to get it on, they stripped down and raced for Neil's king-sized bed, where they rough-housed like a couple of alley cats and tried to wrestle each other into submission. They kept at it for a good five minutes until, under an unrelenting hail of hot passionate kisses, Ricky let himself be pinned. Neil quickly hunkered down to claim his waiting, massive prize.

"Ahhhhh. Oh, fuuuuuuuck."

Heaven, Neil was in heaven. At last, at long last, Ricky's magnificent club, in all its upright majesty, was his! Like a starved, half-crazed animal he held the throbbing, vein-laced shaft with both hands and hungrily devoured the steaming fuckpole in his wet, willing mouth. It was too big for him to take all of it at once but, with a lot of daring and a few knowing tricks, he soon had Ricky thrashing in the throes of an intense, all-encompassing blowjob.

"Oh, yeah! Oh fuck, yeah!" moaned Ricky. "Suck it! Suck that cock! Suck my big, fucking cock!"

But it wasn't long before Ricky, propelled by Neil's skillful mouth and his own rampant desires, raced perilously close to the point of no return and tried to cool things down a bit. He carefully eased out of Neil's grasp and pushed him back. "Too soon," he panted. "Too soon."

Neil's frustration and disappointment with the situation was short-lived, however. To his surprise and delight, he quickly discovered Ricky wasn't one of those hung studs who lie back and expect others to do all the work. No, after a moment to catch his breath, Ricky slid down and eagerly swallowed Neil's rock-hard seven inches right to the hilt. "Oh fuck, Ricky, yesss!"

Ricky turned out to be one hell of a cocksucker! He worked Neil's cock like an all-day lollipop, tickling the underside with his tongue, squeezing the shaft with the inside of his mouth, teasing the cockhead with his teeth and, for that overall spine-tingling effect, driving up the pressure by twisting away on Neil's ballsac. He soon had Neil racing for the stars and groaning, "No. No. Too soon. Oh God, too soon."

He pushed Ricky off, rolled over between the hunk's hairy, muscular legs and sucked first one big bullnut into his mouth and then the other for a good wash and chew. Plums, they were the size of fucking plums! It took a lot of maneuvering to get both of them in at the same time but seeing Ricky go stark raving bananas made the effort more than worthwhile. "Ah! Oh, yeah! Oh fuck, yeah! Ah! Ahh!"

Fantastic! This was far-fucking fantastic! Neil left a trail of kisses around Ricky's groin, up over his washboard abs and the hard, unyielding musculature of his heaving, curved pecs to the perky little nubs standing like miniature beacons on those pecs, lavishing them with special attention—nipping and biting them with his teeth and tracing them with his tongue—until he had Ricky crying out in sweet, delicious agony. Happier than a pig in shit, he spent a few moments working over the pecs again before heading back down to the throbbing slab of manmeat for more tender, loving attention.

Short of breath and pumped to the max, Ricky pulled Neil up for a long frenzied kiss. Then, like a sinner seeking salvation, he fell on his back, raised his legs in the air to expose his pink, puckered asshole and begged, "Fuck me. Please, fuck me. You got me so hot, I gotta have it. My ass is crying for it, aching for it! Please, Neil, fuck me! Fuck me hard! *Fuck me*!"

"I'll fuck ya," Neil growled. "I'll fuck the piss outta you." He grabbed a condom off the night table and carefully slipped it on his burning, cum-dripping cock.

Sheathed in its slick latex cover, Neil's fuckpole surged in anticipation when he pressed it against Ricky's cute little rosebud. Cute, but tight. Fucking tight. Neil gritted his teeth and pushed to ease his cockhead past the protective sphincter. Finally it gave way and he slid in.

"Ahhhh!" Having established his beachhead, Neil slowly but confidently drove his cock in all the way to his balls, almost crying out in the process as Ricky's tight little hole clamped around his dick like a vise. "Ahhh, fuck, yes!"

"Yeah! Oh fuck, Neil, that feels incredible! You're hot, so fucking hot! Oh God, it feels so good! So fucking good! Now, fuck me, hot man! Fuck me!"

Neil fucked him, alright, long and hard. Fucked that tight little bubblebutt until they were both drenched in sweat and crying out for relief. What an ass! What a fucking hot, tight hole! It grabbed his cock like a clamp and drove him crazy! Hot man! Hot ass! Hot fucking ass!

Suddenly his cock couldn't take it any more. Too hot, too tight! Neil felt the heart-stopping explosion go off in his nuts and, almost as if he were making it his last act on Earth, drove his cock hard and deep into Ricky's hot, smothering ass, where he knew it would do the most good. "Ah! Ahh! Ahhh! Ahhhhh!"

Almost at the same time, Ricky let out a bellow and, bucking like a high-spirited bronc, had a gut-busting orgasm of his own. Without so much as a finger on it, his big horsedick began shooting great gobs of creamy white cum all over his chest and shoulders. Fucking gallons of the stuff in a never-ending barrage! "Ah fuck! Yes! Yes! Yesssss!"

It took a long while for Neil's breathing and pulse rate to get anywhere near back to normal after his incredible workout with Ricky. But that was okay, he didn't mind dozing within the confines of Ricky's strong, muscular arms at all. "I think you deserve to go to the head of the class for that effort," he said finally.

"I was damn good, wasn't I?" smirked Ricky.

"God, your good looks are exceeded only by your arrogance," Neil fumed.

Ricky smiled and gave him a squeeze. "Okay, I admit I couldn't have done it without you, Teach. Now, settle down and get some sleep. You're going to need it tomorrow."

"I am?"

"Yup. I got a *long* way to go before graduation."

Class of '75

TONY GLANCED AT THE banner stretched above the hotel's front desk, "Welcome Back Class of '75," and shuddered. He was not looking forward to this weekend at all. A high-school reunion is a celebration of all that is normal, he reasoned, and since he didn't have a nine-to-five job, a wife, 2.5 kids, or a house in the suburbs, he was anything but normal. How could he possibly talk about his life as an actor, or his world of gay discos, the perfect trick and Fire Island, and make it sound normal? Especially to anyone still living in Kansas?

"Tony! Yoo-hoo, Tony!"

Too late, he was trapped. He switched on his best award-winning smile and turned to face Mary Beth Hoffnagel, social convenor par excellence. After 10 years, she was still wearing the same sweater draped over her shoulders, the same black, horn-rimmed glasses with the pointed rhinestone ends. She was even still carrying a red, plastic clipboard.

"Oh, Tony," she bubbled, "I'm so glad you could come. Imagine you, a big Hollywood star!"

"Well, one small role in a low-budget picture hardly makes me—"

"And you're on television too!"

"Occasionally . . . small roles. . . . It always takes a while to—"

"You're just doing so well for yourself."

"Hey, Tony! Tony!" It was Charlie Dawson, class putz and all-around jerk. "That sure was a great deodorant commercial!"

Tony's frozen smile masked gritted teeth. *I play Iago off-Broadway to rave reviews, and all this clown can talk about is something I did two years ago*, he fumed. "Still working for your father at the fertilizer plant, Charlie?" Asshole.

"Oh, by the way," chirped Mary Beth, "more people came than we planned, so we had to do some doubling up. If it's all right with you, you'll be sharing a room with Jeb Nordstrom. You remember Jeb, don't you? He plays for one of those professional football teams now. He's done so well for himself. Just like you. Well, I gotta run. Here's a Reunion Welcoming Kit and a schedule for this evening's events. Bye."

Oh God, he thought, *not Jeb Nordstrom*. Tony's stomach tightened. In their Senior year, under the very noses of everyone in town, he and Jeb had carried on a smoldering love affair. Well, for Tony it was love. For Jeb it was probably nothing more than getting his rocks off. The hunky jock constantly reminded him he preferred doing it with girls. He never once let Tony forget who was "the man," and rarely allowed them to be seen together in public. There had been almost as much pain as pleasure in their relationship, but even after 10 years Tony's warm feelings for Jeb hadn't diminished. He had thought he had those feelings under control. He'd been wrong.

Moments later, standing in the middle of their room, Tony felt the knot in his stomach twist tighter as he stared at the sleeping arrangements. *A double bed*, he groaned to himself, *we've got to share a double bed*.

"Do you toss and turn?"

"What?"

Jeb Nordstrom, buck naked and dripping wet, stood framed in the bathroom doorway. "In your sleep. That bed ain't very big."

"I was just thinking that." Exactly as he had feared, the longer Tony stared at the 6′1″ blond hunk, the more his emotions surged within him. Jeb still had the innocent farmboy face with the cobalt-blue eyes and winning smile, but now his body had *man* stamped all over it: broad shoulders, chiseled pecs, molded arms, defined wasp-waist and sinewy legs. Jeb obviously took very good care of himself.

Tony felt his mouth go dry as he focused on the dangling monster at Jeb's crotch. The thick chunk of cut meat, pushed forward by the large nutsac slung behind it, seemed to hang halfway to Jeb's knees. Soft, it was so fat and plump it didn't seem human; erect it was a lethal 10-inch pillar of rock-hard manmeat.

Standing there, Tony had an odd sense of deja vu. It was as if the two of them were suddenly back in the deserted high-school locker room more than 10 years ago. Tony had just finished drying himself when he turned to find Jeb, dripping wet and sporting a raging hard-on, watching him from the doorway to the showers.

The hair along the back of Tony's neck rose when Jeb started walking towards him, a beginning smirk on his face, his hips thrust forward, accentuating the ponderous back-and-forth swing of his clublike cock. He stopped some five feet away and set one foot up on a bench. Then, in total control, he deliberately slid both hands down the length of his torso, over his molded pecs and washboard abs, over his hairy crotch and throbbing tool, until he had pushed the straining organ all the way down between his legs. Suddenly the cock broke free and snapped back against Jeb's stomach with a loud "thwack!"—giving Tony a start and bringing a smile to Jeb's lips.

Jeb slowly, lovingly stroked his meat a few times before placing his hands confidently on his hips. "Go ahead, take it," he whispered. "You know you want it."

Licking his parched lips, Tony hesitated only a moment before kneeling in front of Jeb's pulsing member and gingerly taking it in his hands, he opened his mouth, leaned forward and—

"Tony! Jeb! It's me, Mary Beth! I know you're probably hashing over old times in there, but the Reunion Welcome Back Cocktail Party started 10 minutes ago!"

Jeb scowled briefly at the interruption and then, still fondling his straining erection, gave Tony a shy, boyish grin. "I missed you, babe."

The Welcome Back Cocktail Party wasn't as much of an ordeal as Tony had thought it would be. In fact, once he got into it, he rather enjoyed seeing his former classmates. And for their part, they seemed more interested in whether he knew any movie stars than why he wasn't married.

Only once did the situation get tense, when Charlie Dawson asked him in front of a large group if it weren't true that most actors were fags. Inwardly, Tony died a slow death and frantically tried to think of a snappy comeback. To his surprise, it was Mary Beth who jumped to his defense, saying it was only a lot of *National Enquirer* bunkum, that there were lots of heterosexual actors, and what did it matter even if it were true? To which Jeb added that he'd heard rumors there were fags even in pro football! Well, nobody believed *that* one, and suddenly everyone was talking about last year's Super Bowl.

"Fags, even in pro football," chuckled Tony, fumbling for his watch on the bedside table. "Imagine that." It was 8:30 a.m. He started to stretch, to work out the kinks of a restless night, when a thick, corded arm wrapped around his waist and pulled him into a warm, muscular body.

"Where do you think you're going?"

"Nowhere, I guess." Something hard and hot brushed against the crack of Tony's ass, and at once his breath quickened in anticipation. Reaching behind him, he felt for Jeb's straining 10 inches. "Oh, fuck!"

It was so fucking big! The size of it never ceased to amaze him. It was more than a cock, it was a weapon. He ran his fingers along the shaft, long and straight and almost as thick as his wrist, until he came to the plum-sized cockhead, silky-smooth and already dripping precum from its gaping pisshole. "Oh, fuck."

Jeb pulled a jar of lube from his bedside table and started slapping it on. "Ten years, Tony, I've waited 10 years for this. You're the—"

"Are you going to talk or are you going to fuck?" chided Tony. He reinforced the question by pressing his waiting, itchy hole against the slicked head of Jeb's erection. He was ready!

Even after relaxing as much as possible, Tony still found the size of Jeb's meat a strain. "Oh God," he groaned, as the bulging cockhead slowly, ever-so-slowly, squeezed past his greased sphincter. "You're so fucking big!"

"Easy, babe, easy. . . . That's it. . . . Oh man, that feels so good. Easy, babe, we're almost there. . . . Oh man, it feels—"

"So good! Oh fuck, I missed this . . . ah-h-h-h. . . . You're in, Jeb, all the way, I can tell. . . . I feel like I'm going to explode . . . ah-h-h. . . . That's it, yes. . . . Now, fuck me, stud. Fuck me hard, just like you used to!"

"You bet I'll fuck you. I'll ride you so hard you'll—"

"Jeb! Tony! Yoo-hoo, are you in there?"

Tony's eyes widened in disbelief. "Oh please," he whimpered, "not *now*, Mary Beth."

"Are you up?"

"In more ways than one, Mary Beth," snarled Jeb, holding in midstroke.

"What?"

"We're up, Mary Beth, we're up!" Tony hoped he sounded cheery enough so she'd go away.

"Are you decent?"

"No, we're not, you stupid cow. I'm lying here with my cock up Tony's—"

"Uh, no we're not," Tony broke in. "We're, um, still dressing."

"Still dressing? You boys are worse than a couple of women. I'll give you just two minutes. You're missing the Reunion Breakfast. Come on, let's get those cute little tushes in motion and not keep everyone waiting. You heard me, come on!"

"My tush was in motion," sighed Tony.

Like a piece of limp sausage, the last of Jeb's cock slipped out of Tony's ass. "This is worse than training camp," he grumbled. Leaning over, he gave Tony a long, loving kiss full on the mouth and said, "I promise I'll make it up to you."

Tony couldn't hide his surprise. "You kissed me. On the lips. You never used to do that."

"I never used to do a lot of things," replied Jeb. And then he kissed Tony full on the mouth again.

Late afternoon found Tony dozing in a chair by the pool. He was dressed for jogging, but somehow his "get up and go" had left without him. He was quite comfortable sitting there doing nothing when a hand nudged his shoulder. He opened his eyes to find Jeb's meat-laden shorts level with his mouth. He couldn't help smiling lasciviously. "You know, in some states you could be charged with carrying a concealed weapon."

"It ain't called The Dick of Death for nothing," Jeb smirked. "Come on, let's get out of here. I'm going to snap if I have to look at one more wallet full of kiddie pictures."

That was all the urging Tony needed. They soon had the hotel far behind them, and in less than half an hour were standing before their old high school, laughing and swapping stories. To their surprise and delight, Old Man Cruikshank, the school's custodian, was there. He not only remembered them as students but revealed how avidly he followed their professional careers, even quoting from a review of Tony's Iago to prove it.

Cruikshank apologized for not being able to stay longer but insisted they have a look around for old time's sake anyway. "You boys are big enough not to do anything you shouldn't," he winked.

"Just close this door when you leave."

Once alone, Jeb couldn't help laughing out loud. "Us boys are big enough to know *exactly* what to do."

"I still can't get over the fact that Cruikshank reads theater reviews," replied Tony. "I never would have thought—"

"I never would've thought I'd finally get you alone," Jeb cut in. "I was getting tense."

"You were getting horny," corrected Tony. He reached down and cupped the bulge in Jeb's jockstrap. "You *are* horny."

"Yeah, my concealed weapon ain't so concealed any more." He put an arm around Tony's shoulders. "This way."

The locker room was cool, damp and musty. No amount of airing or disinfectant would ever dispel the odor of sweat, liniment and dirty jockstraps. It brought back a lot of memories for Tony, and his cock hardened in response.

In seconds, Tony and Jeb were naked and locked in a tight embrace. Their hard cocks were mashed tightly between their writhing bodies as their tongues explored the hidden regions of their mouths—probing, searching, triggering a thousand different sensations. Their kisses peppered each other's necks, shoulders, chests and stomachs; nipples hardened, puckered, were nipped until the recipient cried out in pain and delight; bellies were licked, ear lobes nibbled and throats slavishly tongued.

Jeb reached behind, grabbed the cheeks of Tony's rounded ass and began massaging the firm flesh in his bearlike hands. When Tony grunted at the unexpected force and clenched his muscles in response, Jeb growled, "Yeah, fight me, babe, fight me. Fight me with your smooth, tight ass."

"Fuck me," gasped Tony, "fuck me."

"Not yet, babe. Too soon." Jeb picked Tony up, stood him on a bench and quickly swallowed Tony's raging hard-on right to the balls.

Tony almost buckled at the knees, the suction on his cock was so intense. Jeb seemed to know instinctively what it would take to drive him wild. Just when Tony thought he was going to race over the brink, Jeb straightened and smiled.

"Can't have you going off yet, not until I've got you where I want you."

Tony bent and kissed Jeb long and full on the lips, then sat down on the bench, took a deep breath and slowly devoured Jeb's erect 10 inches, starting with the bulbous, silky-smooth head and working back along the thick shaft. He started slowly, but it wasn't long before he had worked himself into a cocksucking frenzy. He kept pouncing on the rock-hard column, drawing as much of the awesome meat into his mouth as he could, slaving over the huge cockhead, tickling the glans with his tongue and pulling on the slippery outer skin with his lips, all the while stroking the fat shaft jackhammer-style with his hand.

"Oh-h-h, fu-u-u-ck," Jeb moaned. "I can't . . . hold . . . Ah! Ah! Oh fuck . . . Yes-s-s-s-s-s-s!"

Tony could feel the sudden contraction, the rush of blood and then—*bam!*—the first wad of thick, syrupy cum rocketed up the shaft and exploded within his mouth. He quickly sucked the wad down and was hit by a second and then a third. It was as if Jeb had been saving his manseed for just this reunion and was now going to drown Tony in a sea of cum.

"Oh fuck, yes!" roared Jeb, as he pumped his exploding cock deep into Tony's eager, waiting mouth. "Yes! Yes! Yessss!"

With barely time to catch his breath, Jeb dropped to his knees and pounced on Tony's throbbing hard-on, sucking for all he was worth, working on it like an animal possessed. Tony reached down, found Jeb's puckered nipples and was rewarded with a deep, satisfying groan the moment he started playing with them.

In minutes, Tony was gasping for air and shaking his head, trying to ward off the impending climax. With the incredible tension his cock was under it wouldn't take—"Oh geez, Jeb . . . I . . ."

Jeb quickly got to his feet and, between hot and heavy kisses, gasped, "Fuck me, Tony, you gotta fuck me!"

"You want me to—?"

"You heard me. I want that big, fat dick of yours right up my ass, fucking the living daylights out of me. I want your hot cum right up my ass."

"You never—"

"But I do now!" After a long, passion-filled kiss, Jeb looked Tony in the eye and said, "What can I say? A lot can happen in 10 years. Yes, I admit it, I'm a confirmed faggot. There'll be no more denials, no more holding back. OK? Now, will you please take that hot, mean-looking dick of yours and shove it up my fucking ass? I've been dreaming about this moment for a long, long time."

"All right!" Tony gave Jeb one last kiss before spinning him around, bending him over a bench, thrusting his spit-slicked cock between the parted muscular asscheeks into the waiting pink hole.

"Yes-s-s-s!" groaned Jeb. "Oh, yes-s-s-s-s!"

There was no technique in what followed, no grace and little consideration. None was wanted, none given. What ensued was pure, mindless, animal fucking at its basest level, the release of pent-up needs and desires, the fulfillment of a myriad of dreams and fantasies.

Tony fucked for all he was worth, pounding again and again into Jeb's eager ass. Sweat poured off him in rivers as an invisible hand gripped Tony's nuts and sent him reeling to his detonation point. "You want it, Jeb? You got it!"

"Uh! Uh! Oh, yeah! Fuck me, Tony, fuck me! It feels . . . so . . . good!"

"Uh! Ah! Jeb! Jeb, I'm . . . Oh fuck!"

"That's it, babe! Shoot! Cum inside me! Fill me with your hot, heavy cum! I want it, I want all of it!"

"Ah! Ah!" A bomb went off in Tony's nuts. "Ah! Ah! Yes!" He went rigid, head back, his mouth open wide in a long, silent scream. Then—*bam!*—the first wad of red-hot jism burst from his balls, raced up his shaft and shot deep within Jeb's heaving belly. Tony snapped back to life and started pounding for all he was worth. Pounding and pounding and pounding!

"Yes-s-s-s, that's it!" shouted Jeb. "That's it!"

"Ah-h-h-h-h-h!"

"Yes-s-s-s-s-s-s!"

It was long past dinner before Tony and Jeb, hungry, tired and thoroughly fucked-out, finally made it back to the hotel. Who should catch them sneaking through the lobby but Mary Beth Hoffnagel.

"Jeb! Tony! Where on earth have you been? You missed the banquet completely and we had to start the Sweetheart Dance without you!"

"That's okay." Jeb openly winked at Tony. "I've got my sweetheart."

Blushing beet-red, Tony stammered, "We'll, uh, hurry and get changed, Mary Beth, and be, uh, right down."

"OK, but don't take too long." Mary Beth was turning to go when, suddenly, she stopped dead in her tracks and peered reprovingly over her shoulder. "I must admit, I was rather worried there for a while. I thought you two would *never* get together."

"It wasn't for lack of trying, Mary Beth," huffed Tony. Then breaking into a wide grin, he repeated, "It sure wasn't for lack of trying."

The Muscle Shoppe

THE FIRST TIME I saw Jesse I almost plowed into the back end of a Cadillac. Seriously. I was pulling into the parking lot of a suburban strip mall and happened to glance over at my intended destination, a store called The Muscle Shoppe, when I spotted the short, stocky, strikingly handsome young Asian hunk standing just outside the store's front door.

He wore a baggy, oversized sweatshirt but I knew from experience that it took a lot of muscle to fill a shirt out the way he did. What really caught my eye, though, was the size and fit of his spandex shorts (very small and very tight) compared with the size and shape of his bare, densely-muscled legs (very large and incredibly defined). The sight was quite startling—and intensely erotic—and for a moment I was totally oblivious to anything else. It was only by the sheerest dumb luck that my attention snapped back to the road in time for me to slam on the brakes. I stopped barely an inch from the Caddie. The old biddy behind the wheel was none too pleased but my only concern was catching up with the hunk.

I parked the car as quickly as I could and dashed into The Muscle Shoppe in a frantic bid to find the sexy stud. Imagine my surprise and delight when I walked in and he was behind the counter talking on the phone. He worked there! Not only that but he apparently worked there alone. I couldn't believe my good fortune. He smiled a hello but continued fielding questions from his phone-in customer, which was fine by me because it gave me a chance to check out both the store and the man himself.

The store, I got to admit, was really incredible. It billed itself as having "Everything for Your Bodybuilding Needs" and, from what I could see, that was right. You name it, the store sold it: weights and lifting equipment, vitamins and supplements, workout clothes, books, magazines, novelties and knickknacks. The variety and selection were staggering.

The man behind the counter was staggering, too. In his early twenties, he was about five foot five tall and weighed in the neighborhood of 160 very muscular pounds. He had light-brown skin the color of burnished teak, a round boyish face under the trendy black crewcut, dreamy dark-brown eyes behind wire-framed glasses, a broad smile (with dimples yet!) and dazzling white teeth. I was completely captivated by his shape, charisma and blatant sex appeal. As tacky as this sounds, having had little contact with Asian men, either while growing up (a small, almost exclusively white, Midwest town) or in adult life (even though I lived in a major West Coast city for years), up until that moment I had never looked at Asian men sexually. This hot'n'humpy fellow opened my eyes and changed all that.

He finished talking on the phone and came over to see if I needed any help. To be honest, I found him a little over-powering at first. Sure, he was outgoing and friendly, but his high energy and brimming self-confidence (ah, youth) also made him a mite too earnest and aggressive for my liking. Not only that, he was real chatty. I hate chatty salespeople. They're often superficial and interested only in making a sale. Who needs them?

But the diminutive hunk (maybe I should mention I'm six foot one, weigh 195 pounds and have spent years pumping iron myself—hence the continual references to size differentials) was a persistent and engaging charmer who never gave up. He slowly broke through all my natural defenses, finding out that I was new in town (job transfer), single, disliked bars, and had yet to find a gym. He also complimented my physique, scowling when I joked, "Yeah, not bad for an old fart," and insisted I try his gym.

Not sure where Jesse (we had exchanged names early on) was coming from (I mean, it was possible he was just an overly friendly straight guy starved for conversation) I started out fairly neutral. But once bewitched by his captivating charm, I soon threw caution to the wind and became quite open and utterly shameless. I found out he was 24 (ten years my junior!), born in Manila but raised locally, loved working-out (and had competed in the past), wanted his own business, also disliked bars and, like me, was still single. "A hot, muscular, sociable stud like you?" I marvelled. Okay, okay, so I laid it on a little thick.

As obvious as a Mack truck about my interest in him, I honestly didn't hold out much hope of anything happening between us.

There were just too many years, too many differences, too many . . . well, you get the picture. I figured I'd just relax, enjoy his marvelous company and soak in the view. I was absolutely taken by his engaging, boyish face (I've always been a sucker for crewcuts and dimples), lusted for what was under the sweatshirt and spandex (was it my imagination or did Jesse have a hard-on?), and salivated over those smooth monster thighs.

It was when he said he found it difficult to get dates and thought it might be because of his race that the ground shifted. I immediately leapt to his defense and said, "There's still a lot of intolerance out there, Jesse. But don't worry. You're a very good-looking, gregarious kind of guy. With everything you've got going for you, sooner or later you're going to meet someone special and charm the pants right off them." Good, solid, big brotherly advice, I thought.

Jesse looked me in the eye and, with a lascivious grin, said, "I think you're special. Very special. I'd really like to charm the pants off you."

I felt my face turn beet-red. Damned if I hadn't walked into an ambush of my own design! The mini-mountain of muscle was good. Real good. And, omigod, I could see now that he did have a hard-on! A good solid four inches with a cut, walnut-sized head was clearly outlined through the blue and white striped spandex. Flustered, I tried to change the subject. "Those are very impressive legs, Jesse. You must do a lot of squats."

"I'd like to squat over your face," he replied, not missing a beat. Smiling at my continued embarrassment, he added, "I like working my legs. That's why I wear these shorts. They're very small and tight and really show off my big, buffed thighs."

Desperately trying to regain my composure I joked, "Jesse, they are so small and tight they show off everything. Your legs, your ass, your . . . everything."

Stroking his hard cock through the spandex, Jesse frowned and said, "I wish my everything was bigger. Just another couple of inches. Maybe that's why I don't get dates."

I reached over and put a firm hand on Jesse's crotch. "It looks and feels big enough to me." Our eyes locked mere inches from each other and I started rubbing the red-hot erection. "Size does not make the man," I intoned. A platitude, I know, but true.

Less than a minute later, with my fingers doing their thing on his dick, Jesse suddenly lost control and shot a hefty load of thick warm cum into the spandex-lined cup formed by the palm of my hand. Despite his calm exterior, the poor guy must have been so tense and excited inside that it had taken only a few strokes to get him off. I have to admit, instead of being disappointed or ticked off by his lack of control, I was rather taken by his boyish exuberance.

We would have stayed like that a long time, my hand on his crotch, gazing lustfully into each other's eyes, if a car's horn hadn't snapped us back to reality.

Jesse took a deep breath and whispered, "Wow, that was definitely a magic moment." He glanced at his watch and said, "Don't go away." In no time he locked the front door, turned out the lights (making it dim but not dark), and fetched his gym bag from behind the counter.

"Aren't you closing a little early?" I asked.

"Half an hour," he replied.

"And you won't get into trouble?"

He flashed that lascivious smirk again and said, "Shouldn't be a problem. But if it is, it'll be worth it." He grabbed a towel from his gym bag and tossed it to me. "Here, help me clean up."

With that, Jesse peeled off the spandex and shed it like a second skin, offering up his perfectly proportioned circumcised cock (still semi-erect, I might add), dangling peanut-sized ballsac and breathtaking bubblebutt for my inspection and gratification. The left side of his crotch and most of the cute little black pubic patch was smeared with an utterly amazing amount of creamy-white cum.

"Geez, what a mess, Jesse," I said admiringly.

"Big load, huh?" he grinned. "Don't worry, there's plenty more where that came from."

"I'll bet there is," I grinned back.

I got down on my knee and, towel in hand, eagerly went about Jesse's clean-up. I barely touched him and his cock sprang to its full, rock-hard dimensions. Rubbing the rough terrycloth over and around his throbbing dick caused a multitude of minor body tremors and brought a wonderful, low moan rumbling from his belly. Doing the same to his sensitive, low-slung balls made him drop into a half-squat so that his nuts were exposed for even easier access and caused him to groan like a cat in heat. It was beautiful. So beautiful I kept at it long after I'd cleaned up the last of the spunk.

"Whoa, is it just me or is it real warm in here?" gasped Jesse. He pulled the sweatshirt over his head and threw it aside. His smooth teak-colored skin was glistening with perspiration. It gave his brawny, muscular torso a warm, rich sheen.

I couldn't resist any longer. I tossed the towel and, holding on to his curved, satin-smooth buttcheeks for support, pounced on Jesse's erect, bite-sized cock with my hungry, manipulative mouth. With its comfortable size and yummy features, I made a real meal of it. Hell, let's be honest, I devoured it. And let me tell you, Small *is* Beautiful. Especially when it's attached to a hot, responsive man like Jesse.

He went crazy. Between sucking on his cock, yanking on his balls and deep-massaging that muscular butt of his, I had Jesse revved in no time. He loved every minute and was very vocal and appreciative of what I was doing (he's got the sexiest, deepest groan). That, of course, encouraged me to work even harder.

Just when I thought I had him, Jesse yanked his cock from my mouth and hauled me to my feet. "Not yet. No, not yet," he gasped. "Too soon. Too soon!"

Well, Jesse wasn't the only one revved up and rarin' to go. I took one look at his full, soft pliable lips and dove in for some serious, heavy-duty lip-lock. I love to neck. I can kiss/neck/spoon/whatever for hours. Well, damned if it wasn't one of Jesse's favorite activities, too. And man, did he know how to use his tongue! Trouble was, we revved so fast we raced right out of control again.

Jesse practically tore my clothes right off, he was so eager to get me naked. Between the deluge of kisses he lavished on my lips, he kept moaning, "You are so hot. You are so-o-o hot. You are *so hot!*" That's the pot calling the kettle black, I thought.

Then, once he had me bareassed, he couldn't keep his hands off. They roamed everywhere. Over my shoulders, arms, chest and abs; over my back, ass, cock and balls. Pressing, squeezing, pinching, pulling and massaging. He stoked the fire and pushed us both even closer to the edge.

I brought my hands up and laid them on his squared, rock-solid pecs. He flexed them for me, proudly showing off the mass, density and definition of his hard-won musculature. I squeezed back, letting him know I was impressed. I bent forward and took first one soft, virgin-smooth nipple in my mouth, then the other. I sucked and licked and nibbled on the little brown nubs until I had them pumped to the max and sensitized to even the slightest touch. He couldn't get enough nipple play and kept begging for more. And more. And still more. Then he did the same to me, driving me crazy with his enthusiastic titwork. I was practically delirious by the time he moved on.

Or should I say, moved lower? Jesse blazed a trail of kisses down my chest and abs, nuzzled for a moment in the thatch of my pubic hair and then, holding onto it with both hands, pounced on my throbbing, cum-dripping cock with the ferocity of a tiger. What he lacked in ability (his little mouth couldn't take much more than the head and an inch or two of my shaft—and I don't have a huge cock) he more than made up for with heart, desire and tenacity. It was like he hadn't sucked cock in a long, long time! And when he wasn't actually sucking on my dick, he was either jacking me off or playing with my balls. It was incredible.

Incredible got even better when he sat me down on a padded bench, knelt between my legs and pounced a second time. My cock never had it so good. Every now and then I'd force his head up and we'd indulge in some serious lip-lock, which gave me a chance to show him my appreciation, but he seemed committed to ravaging my cock and didn't stray too far from it for long. Fine by me. I returned his effort by reaching under and playing with his nipples. He really loved that.

Jesse kept up the oral assault on my energized dick until, somehow, he sensed I was very close to losing it. Breaking free, he raced to his gym bag and returned with a condom and a tube of lube. "Please put this on," he gasped. "I want you to fuck me."

He could see I was somewhat taken aback by this sudden turn of events.

"I'm not a slut. I don't bend over for just anyone. Honest. But I want to bend over for you because you're"—and Jesse became unusually reticent—"you're my fantasy man."

Excuse me? I couldn't believe my ears. Here was a hot young stud—who was probably being chased all over town by other hot young studs—telling me I was his fantasy man! If anyone else had used a line like that on me, I would have burst out laughing but, I don't know, there was something about the way Jesse said it that caught me totally off-guard. I had the definite feeling that, at that exact moment, he was telling the absolute truth.

He looked me dead in the eye and with a deep growl begged, "Please."

"Jesse, I'm very flattered," I stammered. "And I'd love to fuck you silly but, well . . . I know I'm not exactly hung like a horse but I think I still might be just a little too big for a man of your, um, stature.'

Jesse actually blushed. "Don't worry. I've been practicing at home with a dildo that's about the same size as your cock. You know, just in case I was to actually meet my fantasy man."

He stared at me, waiting. I stared back, immobilized. He smiled. I smiled. He grinned. I grinned. My erection got bigger and harder and then, I don't know, there was a cosmic flash and I blurted out, "Okay, yes! Let's do it!"

I got up and slipped on the condom while Jesse lay on his back on the padded bench and hoisted his massive thighs up over his chest to offer up the cutest little puckered butthole nestled between the sexiest, most mouth-watering curved asscheeks you ever saw in your entire life. It was a beautiful, beautiful sight and my cock surged to epic proportions. I slicked my latex-sheathed poker and squeezed the rest of the gel over the waiting portal. I ran my forefinger around the pursed buttlips and Jesse squirmed expectantly under my touch.

Gently I positioned my cock against the little rosebud. God, it looked so small compared to my dick! I pushed against the sphincter, popped the seal and carefully slid inside. I took it real slow and easy (I could tell by the grimace on Jesse's face that, trooper though he was, it still hurt like hell) but I didn't let up until I was all the way in and my electrified, cum-laden balls were pressed against his hard bubblebutt. I leaned forward and gave him a long, serious kiss. It took his mind off the pain and gave him a chance to get used to me filling his ass.

We came up for air for a moment and Jesse exclaimed, "You are so hot! You are such a hot man!"

Ditto, I thought. Ditto. Ditto. And more ditto.

I started fucking with a series of long, easy strokes. "Ohhh, yess-s-s-s," moaned Jesse. I could tell the pain was being slowly transformed into spine-tingling, mind-expanding ecstasy the more Jesse relaxed and let himself go. Soon the fuck-hungry mini-muscle-stud was really into it and loudly begging for more. I, ever eager to please, was happy to give him the ride of his ever-lovin' life.

The long, easy strokes gradually became shorter and harder until I was pounding into that tight little hole like a jackhammer into concrete. Jesse's whole body shook under the punishing workout. Each bone-jarring thrust reverberated from the top of his head to the soles of his feet (cute how his little toes were curled up the whole time). From experience, I knew the tortured expression on his face belied the adrenaline rush of the pleasure-pain radiating from his ass. That inspired me to go harder and faster still.

Jesse insistently urged me on with a continual litany of grunts, groans and moans. He also barked out a steady stream of words. It was pretty basic, but he got his feelings across: 'Yes! That's it! Harder! Deeper! That's it! I feel it! Fuck me! Let me feel it! Oh man, this is so wonderful! Yessss!"

It seemed the more Jesse got, the more Jesse wanted. He was an insatiable, sex-crazed tiger! Not only that, but his hole was so hot and hungry it had a life of its own and I knew, what with the way it was gripping my cock, that I wouldn't be able to hold out much longer. *Bam!* An invisible hand suddenly took hold of my nuts, squeezed them real tight, and detonated the high-octane love-juice simmering between my legs. "Oh fuck yes!"

I blew big-time. A bomb went off in my ballsac and my nuts exploded, sending what felt like a gallon of cum rocketing up my electrified shaft. I shoved my cock in as deep as I could and embarked on a heart-stopping, mind-blowing orgasm of truly epic proportions. "Yesssssssss!"

It got better. Turned out Jesse was closer to losing it than I thought. About halfway through my own fireworks display, I reached over and pinched the sensitized little nubs decorating his rippling pecs. His tits were the trigger. He let out a loud moan, arched his back and suddenly rocketed into a high orgasmic orbit. Without so much as a finger on it, his rock-hard cock pumped out a simply awesome amount of creamy-white cum (he wasn't joking when he said, "there's plenty more where that came from") while his humpy muscular body jerked and bucked its way through a heavy-duty, gut-busting orgasm that made my heart-stopper seem kind of puny in comparison. It was incredible, the stuff of legends.

"Ahhhhhhhhhhhhhhhh."

After that, it took us both a long time to get anywhere near back to normal—normal being a relative term, of course. First we cuddled on the floor, happily content to just hold each other's warm, sweaty body and revel in the company of a kindred spirit. Then Jesse insisted on giving me a relaxing, all-over massage. With a hot stud like him working you over, a massage is anything but relaxing. I returned the favor but darned if the humpy little hunk didn't end up shooting yet another load. (I barely touched him and he got a hard-on, I swear!)

By the time we finished playing, it was quite late and we were both tired and very hungry. I helped Jesse clean up the store and then we went back to my place for dinner. As you can imagine, we ended up doing more than just eating. In fact, Jesse never got home that night.

That was six months ago and it's been crazy ever since. Crazy. And incredible. And exciting. And wonderful. And . . . well, I think you get the idea. Six months and we're still as smitten as ever.

Smitten? Did I say smitten? Believe me, smitten ain't half of it.

Mr. Collegiate

"WE'RE MIGHTY PROUD to have a title-winning bodybuilder training at The Adonis," boasted the gym manager, for something like the third time in ten minutes, as he finished filling out the last of the forms. The title-winning bodybuilder was all he had talked about since Brett signed up and, impressive though the guy might be, he was starting to get on Brett's nerves.

Not that Brett didn't get off on bodybuilders. Far from it, he creamed his jeans every time he passed a set of sharp, defined muscles. But this title-winning number sounded just too good to be true. And if he was true, what was the point in hearing about him because he'd either be super-straight or already busy with a long string of guys?

"Yup, even though he's a senior and could train on campus, Chuck comes here. Says it's too crowded on campus. Says there's too many of them cocksuckers in the showers."

That did it. "Yeh, got to watch out for those cocksuckers," agreed Brett. "Them cocksuckers are everywhere!"

"Remember what I told you," snapped the manager. "Don't get in Chuck's way and don't do anything to get him mad. He really takes his training seriously and he doesn't like people disturbing him. I've seen him get real nasty if he thinks someone is goofing around."

Brett picked up his gym bag and headed for the locker room. "All this hassle just to lift a few weights. Maybe I *should* try the gym on campus."

"My advice is don't even look at him when you're in there!"

Ticked off by the lecture, a slow fuse burned within Brett as he changed into jock, shorts, T-shirt and sneakers. "Some guy wins one rinky-dink, two-bit state muscle contest and everyone treats him like he's God's gift to bodybuilding."

He yanked the door to the weight room open, spoiling for a fight, and snorted, "All I can say is he better look damn good!"

Standing just inside, hands on hips, Brett slowly peered around the cavernous room. What with all the old barbells, dumbbells and black rubber mats strewn about, the gym looked more like a medieval torture chamber than a place to stay in shape. But, then, that was one of the reasons Brett decided to join The Adonis in the first place. It wasn't like one of those sterile uptown health clubs with plush carpeting and racks of shiny chrome weights. It had some character, a kind of gruff, ballsy charm. A real man's gym. Just the place for a twenty-two year-old stud to keep his sleek, head-turning physique in top form.

"Okay, so where is this Mr. Collegiate, who I'm supposed to avoid like the plague?" Brett knew it was only nine-thirty in the morning, but he hadn't expected the place to be deserted. He cursed his new job for making him work out so early, thus missing all the hunks who exercised at night.

Catching a glimpse of white T-shirt, his eyes locked on a moving form. But, no, it was only a mousey executive-type, who looked like he'd get a hernia bending over to tie his shoes.

"Well, it's definitely not him," Brett sniffed, watching as the man stumbled nervously among the weight racks looking for something he could handle.

"Oh, Mr. Collegiate! Come out, come out, wherever you are!" Just then, out of the corner of his eye, Brett caught sight of moving skin and turned for a better look.

"Oh, fuck!" Brett's smug grin slipped off his face, his mouth went dry and thousands of butterflies took off in his stomach. After whistling softly, he nodded and sighed, "Now, there is a bodybuilder!"

Brett and Chuck were about the same height but from there on they were as different as night and day. Where Brett had dark hair and brown eyes, Chuck was blond and blue-eyed; where Brett gave the impression of a lithe, agile gazelle, Chuck immediately conjured up visions of a massive Bengal tiger.

Massive was certainly the word to describe Chuck. He must have weighed at least 200 pounds, maybe 210. And all of it solid muscle. It was incredible how much he had packed on that frame of his. Mind-boggling.

At that moment Chuck was doing curls with about a hundred pounds so intensely that he looked like a man possessed. The effort of pumping heavy iron showed in his pain-wracked face, in his contorted muscles flushed with oxygen-enriched blood and by the gallons of sweat pouring off his body. His ragged T-shirt and shorts clung so snugly they were like a second skin and did little to hide the development beneath them.

That development didn't stop with hard, rippling muscles, either. Even from a distance, Brett could clearly see that Chuck's jock was having a tough time containing the swollen meat in its pouch and he could only guess at how big the thing was fully erect after going through some pumping of its own. He had a feeling that Chuck's cock would be in perfect proportion with the rest of his body, a real prize-winner. Just thinking about the possibilities gave Brett a surging hard-on.

With a grunt, Chuck finished his set and dropped the barbell to the mats. If he was pleased with himself, he sure didn't look it. In fact, he looked like he was in one very bad mood.

"What the hell are you staring at, faggot?"

Brett was caught so much by surprise that he didn't realize at first that Chuck was yelling at the mousey executive and not at him.

"I catch you watching me one more time, faggot, and I'll re-arrange that face of yours! You got that?"

"Oh, geez," groaned Brett. "The guy's a redneck. Well, so much for getting it on with him. If there's one thing I do not need, it's having my face re-arranged."

The mousey executive must have thought the same thing. As fast as he could without actually running, he picked up his towel and made for the door, followed all the way out by Chuck's scowling gaze. It never occurred to Brett that he was going to be standing in Chuck's line of vision until—bam!—Chuck had him in those flashing, angry eyes of his.

"Oh, oh." Brett felt his knees start to buckle and tried a quick smile to show that he was the friendly type. Then, before Chuck could say anything threatening, he hurriedly walked over to a distant corner and started doing push-ups.

All the while he did those push-ups Brett could feel Chuck's eyes boring into him, trying to reach right into the deepest part of his brain, wondering who he was and what he was doing there. It wasn't until he heard the weights clanging in the other corner again that Brett was able to get his breathing anywhere near back to normal. He wasn't easily scared, but his first meeting with Chuck had been downright unnerving!

Brett went to the gym every second morning after that and, to his amazement, Chuck remained as surly as ever. Even after a week, the first thing Chuck did when Brett entered was snarl. Oh, not right to Brett's face, but Brett knew the snarl was for his benefit anyway. The first couple of times the snarl really got to him and he half-expected Chuck to physically attack but, after he got used to it, he simply ignored the greeting, smiled a "hello" of his own, and started in on his warm-ups. He did toy with the idea of snarling back, just to see what would happen, but he never had the guts when the time came to do it.

What became even more frustrating for Brett was knowing that, just as he was interested in Chuck, Chuck was at least mildly curious about him. Right from the first day they fell into a ritual of trying to watch the other without getting caught. The "Sneak-a-Peek Ritual," Brett called it. Easier said than done, he found out.

Brett soon learned the easiest way to sneak a peek was by pretending to look at himself in one of the wall mirrors, then using the mirror to see what Chuck was up to. Even that method wasn't foolproof, though, because nine times out of ten he'd end up catching Chuck trying to sneak a peek of his own. When that happened, Brett couldn't help but grin at him, as if to say, "Gotcha," even though he knew doing it only antagonized Chuck further.

All the games were driving Brett up the wall. It was ridiculous trying to pretend someone he was interested in didn't exist, so he decided the time had come for a little more direct action. He began leaving the protection of his own corner and using equipment all around the gym, even if what he wanted happened to be right next to Chuck.

The first time he walked near the musclestud to get an extra weight, Brett was sure he saw Chuck clench his fists. He dismissed the incident by telling himself, "The guy may be a redneck, but he wouldn't really hit me just because I walked near him."

But when Brett saw the fists involuntarily clench a second time, his eyes widened and he mumbled, "Maybe he would hit me."

Near the end of Brett's workout that same morning it happened that both he and Chuck stopped for a rest only ten feet apart. They leaned stiffly against the wall and stared straight ahead, both pretending the other person wasn't there, both obvious in his discomfort.

Deciding on a frontal attack, his heart pounding in his ears, Brett took a deep breath and casually said, "Man, if it gets any hotter in here, we're going to start frying."

Without acknowledging Brett directly, Chuck replied sarcastically, "If you don't like it, you can always leave."

"I didn't say anything about leaving," smirked Brett. "I just said it was hot."

Chuck pushed himself off the wall and snarled, "I don't talk when I'm working out, asshole." Picking up a barbell, he turned his back and started doing curls.

Fuming, Brett finished his workout in half the time without once bothering to look over at Chuck.

When he finished, Brett let the weight drop to the floor with a deafening crash and angrily stomped to the locker room. With his hand on the door knob, he paused to collect himself and put a big smile on his lips. He turned, looked Chuck right in the eye (he knew he'd be watching him) and in his happiest, cheeriest voice called out, "I'll be seeing you, stud!"

Chuck stopped dead in the middle of a rep. "What the fuck did you call me?"

"And the name's Brett, stud. Call me asshole again and I'll rearrange your face!" Without giving Chuck a chance to reply Brett gave a wave of his hand and walked out.

Two days later, Brett was back. From the minute he walked in he felt Chuck's glaring eyes on him, following his every move, watching his every step. Chuck looked like he'd been chewing a mouthful of nails since their last encounter. Happy he was not.

Still in a feisty mood of his own, though, Brett really didn't give a damn. In fact, deep down, he kind of liked the attention. "At least he's not ignoring me," he kidded himself.

An hour into his workout, while pausing for a rest, Brett couldn't resist looking over to where Chuck was working on the bench press. There must have been at least two hundred and fifty pounds on the bar as Chuck raised it effortlessly from his chest eight times in rapid succession.

"Damn, he's impressive!"

Racking the weight, Chuck stood and walked over to a mirror, where he stripped off his T-shirt and stood relaxed before his reflection, cataloging every plus and minus in his physique. As far as Brett was concerned, Chuck had no minuses. He would have taken him "as is" without a second thought.

Chuck's pumped muscles rippled slightly as he casually shifted his weight from one foot to the other. He didn't yet have the huge size and hardened density that older, more experienced builders possess, but everything there was clearly defined and in perfect proportion. Each muscle had been carefully carved so that it was not only shapely and well-formed but also flowed smoothly into the next, thereby creating the perfect whole. Chuck was nothing short of a Greek statue come to life.

Seemingly satisfied with himself relaxed, Chuck whipped through a few poses to check his flexed musculature. Front double biceps, side chest, abdominal crunch, lats from the front. He looked good, very good.

It was at that point that Brett noticed the bulge in Chuck's jock was bigger than usual—and growing. In fact, it was a miracle how the jockstrap was staying in one piece at all, what with that slab of meat straining against it. Brett couldn't help smiling at the impossible thought of Chuck freeing the engorged flesh and letting it go through a posing routine of its own.

"What the fuck are you staring at, faggot?" Chuck had turned and was facing Brett from a distance of thirty feet, fists clenched.

Brett's first reaction was to lie through his teeth and say he wasn't staring at anything but, surprising even himself, he calmly answered, "You."

Chuck's hands went to his hips. "Why?"

Not flinching for a second, like a gunfighter staring down an opponent, Brett replied, "Because I think you're one hell of a bodybuilder."

Chuck studied Brett a long time before idly scratching his chest and saying, "Is that right? You really get off on muscles, huh? I'll bet you suck cock, too."

Brett nodded. "Yup. Anytime you want to give me a try, just drop your jock."

The sneer melted off Chuck's face. He stood there for something like thirty seconds, looking lost and confused until, finally, pulling himself together, he quickly glanced about to make sure no one else had heard and then growled, "If I wasn't in the middle of my workout, faggot, I might take you up on that."

With that, Chuck grabbed his T-shirt and walked back to his usual corner. He still had his famous scowl but, somewhere along the way, he had lost his swagger.

Brett heaved a deep sigh of relief. "I have got to stop living dangerously."

Deciding it was time to make a tactical retreat, Brett picked up his gear and headed for the locker room. At the door he stopped and turned to face Chuck. "About the blowjob. There's no hurry, it's a standing offer."

Motionless, Chuck returned Brett's gaze for a long time without betraying any of his own emotions. Then, just as it looked like the mask might start cracking, he broke contact, mumbled a quick, "Go fuck yourself," and slid onto the bench for more presses.

Muttering a soft, "Damn," Brett pushed the locker room door open and walked out.

Waking up Monday morning, the idea of lifting weights didn't appeal to Brett at all. In fact, just thinking about barbells caused his stomach to turn. But then, his stomach had been turning all weekend. It was the party after work Saturday night that had done it. Between busting out with new friends and trying to down his unrequited love for Chuck, Brett went out of his way to get smashed. It didn't take long, and he had a lot of fun doing it, but he sure paid for it the next day.

Sunday, Brett didn't even try getting out of bed until late afternoon and, when he did, on the first attempt he got only as far as the bathroom. As for eating, the mere thought of food gave him the dry heaves. "So this is life in the fast lane," he'd tell himself each time his stomach rumbled ominously.

No, it wasn't the desire to pump iron that got Brett to The Adonis Monday morning. It was his determination not to go through another day without seeing Chuck. He figured he'd visit the gym, watch Chuck a while, go through the motions of a workout, then call in sick and collapse. "Oh, the things I do for that guy," Brett murmured.

Striding out of the locker room into the heat of the gym, Brett took one look at Chuck working out in the far corner and knew the effort getting there had been worth it. With his muscles pumped, his bronzed skin glistening with perspiration and his form-fitting shorts straining at the crotch, Chuck was a Herculean fantasy come to life.

"Hmmmm, you can kick sand in my face *anytime*!" whistled Brett, already feeling ten times better.

When Chuck looked over and gave his usual scowl, Brett waved and called out, "Morning, stud!"

"One of these days I really will beat the shit out of you!" roared Chuck, pausing with about three hundred pounds on his shoulders just long enough to deliver his warning.

"Promises, promises," sighed Brett, making his way to his usual warm-up spot. He was so glad he'd kept his gym appointment, he really was feeling better. In rapid succession, he did thirty push-ups and fifty sit-ups.

It must have been the sit-ups. Brett barely finished the last one when the room started spinning and myriads of tiny flashbulbs popped in front of his eyes. For a second he thought he was going to throw up but, mercifully, the churning in his stomach subsided after a few seconds. "Guess there's nothing there," he shrugged.

As soon as he could, Brett gingerly crawled to the nearest wall and leaned back against the rough concrete. Wrapping his arms around his knees, he closed his eyes to wait out the storm and moaned, "This is definitely un-cool."

"Brett?"

It wasn't so much the voice as the gentle squeeze of his shoulder that made Brett open his eyes and slowly lift his head. He was surprised to find Chuck squatting in front of him with concern written all over that handsome, tanned face of his. Brett gave a weak smile. "Hi."

"Hey, you alright?" Gone was the hard, threatening snarl.

"Just a little rough around the edges. Too much vino Saturday night. I'll be alright." Brett tried his best to sound convincing. Not that he wasn't touched at the attention Chuck was unexpectedly giving him, but he was embarrassed at the reason for that attention.

Chuck's eyes probed deeper. "You sure?"

Slowly nodding his head, Brett smiled again. "Positive."

Chuck got up, walked over to his gym bag and rummaged

around in it for a moment. Returning, he tossed an orange in Brett's lap and said, "Eat that, the Vitamin C will do you good."

Then, before Brett could say anything, Chuck pointed a finger at him and snapped, "When you've finished it, get your ass out of here and into bed until you're feeling better! You hear me?"

Striding back to his corner, Chuck shook his head and grumbled, "Shit, the things I have to put up with around here."

"Hey, Chuck!"

The musclestud stopped and, looking royally pissed off, slowly turned to face Brett. "What?"

"Thanks."

Chuck didn't say a word. But the longer he stood there staring into Brett's eyes, the more his scowl disappeared and the more a shy, boyish smile began taking its place. Before it got too big, though, Chuck realized what was happening to him, looked down at his hands and mumbled, "Yeh, well, that's okay." Hesitantly, he turned and made his getaway.

"Gotcha," sighed Brett.

Two days later, Brett was not only back to feeling his normal, chipper self, he was flying! He was high! It was like his whole world had lit up, with brass bands and a sky full of singing birds. The only thing he could think of the whole time he was away was getting back to The Adonis. Back to Chuck. His Chuck.

Chuck, the guy he thought of every day; Chuck, the hunky stud he dreamed of every night; Chuck, who came on like a mean son of a bitch, but whom Brett now knew was warm, caring and feeling. Chuck was the man Brett had been searching for all his life, the man he could spend the rest of eternity with. Now, all he had to do was convince Chuck of the same thing.

Brett was practically delirious by the time he changed into his gym clothes and ran towards the weight room door. He'd been having a long discussion with himself about whether to be obvious and call out, "Morning, stud," when he saw him , or to be low-key and say a simple, "Hey, there." For a second he wished he knew exactly what kind of mood Chuck was in that morning, but then decided it didn't matter because he liked him no matter what mood he was in.

Deciding to go with the "Morning, stud," Brett stepped eagerly into the weight room and looked about for his man. Catching sight of Chuck, he froze dead in his tracks, paralyzed. It was as if an invisible hand had slapped him hard across the face, leaving him stunned and gasping for breath. Unable to stop them, tears started welling in his eyes. "Oh, no! . . . No! . . ."

There was Chuck, laughing and joking and having a great old time, with a bodybuilder Brett had never seen before. Who was he? Where had he come from? What was he doing there now?

The stranger was about the same size as Chuck, but had nowhere near the same amount of density or definition. While he didn't possess Chuck's all-American good looks, he did have a strong animal magnetism that Brett knew could be powerfully attractive. And, dammit, if it didn't look like Chuck had been attracted!

Chuck had just finished a set of donkey raises for his calves and stood hunched over, waiting for the muscular stranger to slide down off his butt. Maybe, just maybe, Brett could have accepted the fact that the guy was only a friend helping Chuck with his workout. But, then, to watch as the stranger guided his crotch along the crack of Chuck's ass and gave him a long, lingering pat on the buns. . . . No, it was just too obvious!

It never occurred to Brett for a second that Chuck might have any sort of life outside the gym, that he might have any close friends or—worst of all—a lover. But the way that stud draped his arm over Chuck's shoulder as they talked told Brett all he needed to know.

Brett was about to turn and walk out when Chuck caught sight of him and, smiling broadly, gave a nod of his head. The stranger twisted round to see who had entered, smirked, and motioned a "Who's he?" to Chuck.

Perhaps it was the stranger's smirk that snapped Brett back to reality but, in a bid to prove to himself and the two bodybuilders that he didn't give a damn about them or what they'd been doing together, he nodded back and grimly walked to his own corner.

Brett tried to bury himself in his workout, to channel his frustration and hurt into pumping as much iron as he could. He vowed to beat his anguish senseless, even if it meant killing himself in the process, but the more iron he lifted the tighter his emotions knotted and twisted. Try as he might, he couldn't get the image of Chuck and "that guy" together out of his mind.

He didn't have to watch them to know they were petting and stroking each other as they went through their workout, he could imagine just how friendly they were getting as they helped one another with their posing routines, and he knew damn well that a hand went down to pat ass every time an "Atta, boy," echoed through the air. It was all so fucking galling! Brett didn't know whether to go over and try beating Chuck to a pulp or bang his own head into the wall for being so blind and stupid!

Hearing Chuck and the stranger saying good-byes and telling each other how much they enjoyed working out together sent Brett into a flurry of exercising. His muscles were sore and knotted like his stomach, but he wasn't going to let on he'd been affected by what had happened in the far corner.

It was only when the stranger called out at last, "See you soon, stud," that Brett almost lost control and looked up. Catching himself, he plowed on with renewed intensity.

Then they were alone. The minutes dragged by and still no sound came from Chuck's corner. "What the hell is he doing?" fumed Brett. Curiosity was making his skin crawl but he wouldn't allow a look, not even a quick peek.

More minutes ticked by. Still no sound.

Turning to add more weight to the barbell, Brett couldn't help himself and glanced over to see what Chuck was doing. To his chagrin, he saw Chuck leaning against a rack watching him. To his even greater annoyance, Chuck smiled and winked at him. Clenching his teeth, Brett found the weight he wanted and went back to his barbell.

Cheerfully, Chuck asked, "Hey, how are you today? Ain't going to throw up, or anything, are you?"

Pausing just long enough to reply, Brett snarled, "You don't have to worry about me. I'm just *fine*!"

"Yeh, so I see. You work that barbell any harder, buddy-boy, and you'll do yourself an injury."

Maintaining his momentum, Brett glared straight ahead and grunted, "Fuck off."

Stung, Chuck waited in puzzled silence until Brett stopped to take a breather. Quickly moving closer, he pulled off his T-shirt, struck a pose that looked something like a discus thrower, and called out, "Hey, Brett! Brett! What do you think about this one?

You think I should use it at the Jr. Mr. State?"

Brett shrugged and looked away. "I don't care."

Chuck became more insistent. "No, come on, tell me."

"Why ask me? What do I know?" snapped Brett. "Your friend with the muscles would be a better person to ask."

Chuck fell out of his pose and stared blankly at Brett. "My friend with the . . . ? Oh, you mean Marty. We were both in the Mr. Collegiate. I know him, but I wouldn't call him a friend. He was here pumping me for training information."

Wide-eyed, Brett wheeled around and was about to roar, "That ain't all it looked like he was pumping you for!" He stopped himself, bit his lip, and turned back to the wall.

Chuck was over to Brett in a flash, clamped a hand on his shoulder and spun him around. "What the hell is going on here?"

Brett made an exaggerated gesture of surprise and let out a loud whoop. "Wow, this really is an occasion! The great Mr. Collegiate has deigned to interrupt one of his all-important workouts to come and fraternize with one of the gym's little people! Well, thanks a bunch, Mr. Collegiate!"

"What the fuck is eating you?"

"Please notice, folks, the friendly way Mr. Collegiate carries on a conversation! With all the charm and tact of a Mack truck hitting a brick wall at 60 miles an hour, he asks, 'What the fuck is eating you?' That's what I like about you, Chuck, you're so damn blunt."

"So, what's wrong with being blunt?"

"Oh, nothing at all! Hey, I'm into blunt. I like blunt! Some people, like your friend, they're into laughing and joking around and having a good time. But me? No, I come here to get my dose of blunt!"

"YOU'RE REALLY ASKING FOR IT, BRETT!"

Throwing up his hands, Brett shouted back, "Hell, I've been asking for it for a long time, Chuck, but it seems I can't match the competition! For weeks now I've tried to get to know you and all I got for my troubles were snarls. But one pat on the ass from Marty, and you turn to jelly! I had my chance and I blew it—no pun intended! So, as they say, to the victor goes the spoils. See you around, Chuck!"

Tirade over, Brett grabbed his gym bag and ran to the locker room, where he stripped off in something like two seconds flat. He was heading to the showers when Chuck came charging through the door like a mad bull and caught him by the arms.

"What the hell is all this talk about victor and spoils? Do you think I want to get it on with Marty?"

"*Bingo*!" exclaimed Brett, fighting to hold back the tears. "Give the man a kewpie doll!"

Chuck's face twisted in frustration and he wailed, "I don't want Marty. I can't stand him, I hate his guts. You're the guy I want. You're the only guy I want! I've wanted you for a long time!"

"Sure you have!" Brett cried.

Without another word, Chuck drew Brett to him and covered his mouth with his own, in a hard, passionate kiss. As the intensity of the long-denied contact grew, he wrapped his arms tightly about Brett and forced his tongue deep into Brett's mouth, exploring each ridge and curve so intensely that he soon had Brett raised to a fever pitch.

Chuck suddenly broke the kiss and, panting heavily, looked imploringly into Brett's eyes. "There, now do you believe me? Now do you believe I want you? Do you want more proof? I'll give you proof!"

Letting go of Brett, Chuck yanked down his shorts and jockstrap and tossed them aside. He straightened to his full height and stood anxiously stroking his nine inches of erect cock. "You want proof?" he asked breathlessly. "I'll give you proof."

Grabbing Brett's hands, Chuck pulled them to his engorged shaft and wrapped them around it. "You want it? It's all yours. You can have it anytime, anywhere you want. Just say the words and it's yours, all yours."

Overwhelmed, Brett didn't know what to say. Finally recovering his senses, he threw his arms around Chuck and planted a hard kiss on the trembling, waiting mouth. How long he stayed like that, Brett didn't know. Time and space melted in the excitement of being in Chuck's arms at last. He wanted Chuck so bad. He wanted all of Chuck.

From his mouth, Brett left a trail of wet kisses down Chuck's neck and over the broad expanse of his chest. He paid particular attention to nibbling and licking the hard, dime-sized nipples and was soon rewarded by Chuck's loud groans of delight.

Between impassioned gasps, Chuck began pleading with Brett and pushing down on his head. "My cock! Suck my cock! My dick is so hot it's going to explode! You gotta . . . You gotta blow me! Please, please blow me!"

Happy to oblige, Brett got down on his knees and pounced on the massive, steaming cock rising before him. Unable to take the whole thing in his mouth at once, he pumped as much of it in and out as he could.

Brett couldn't get enough of that pulsing column! He went into a frenzy as the huge silky-smooth knob slid along the roof of his mouth to the curve of his throat while the throbbing shaft stretched his lips far apart with its width. It was truly a cock fitting Chuck's muscular proportions and Brett had it right where he wanted it!

"Oh, shit!" moaned Chuck, rolling his head from side to side in a futile attempt to try and contain himself. "I can't hold off much . . . I'm coming! I'm . . . !"

Brett felt the welling surge of Chuck's cock, the tight clench of his buns and then his mouth was blasted with what seemed like gallons of searing, sticky cum. Rivers of it. Rivers of the sweetest-tasting cum Brett had ever swallowed. It was like honey! It was like . . . like nothing he'd ever tasted before and yet like everything he knew it would be. It was fantastic!

Shuddering, Chuck dropped to his knees and gave Brett a long, passion-fanned kiss. Then, between light kisses over Brett's face and chest, he panted, "Brett, that was so good, the greatest! But you can't stop now! You can't stop, I won't let you. You got to finish what you started. I'm burning! I'm on fire and you're the only one who can put me out!"

Sliding his hands wildly down the muscular chords of Chuck's shoulders and back, Brett reached Chuck's sweaty, sculpted buns and kneaded them like dough. "How? What do you want me to do? Tell me! Quick, tell me!"

"My ass," moaned Chuck. "You gotta fuck me up the ass!" Falling on his back, Chuck spread his arms along the floor for support and lifted his legs over his chest to give Brett an unobstructed path. "Hurry, I'm hot! I'm on fire! Quick, fill my ass with your cock!"

How long had Brett hoped and prayed for that very moment! Quickly lubing his seven inches with a gob of spit, Brett slid over and pressed the head of his cock against the puckered rosebud. Grabbing Chuck about the waist, he took a deep breath and slowly pulled himself into the hot, tight hole.

Chuck groaned and chewed his lower lip on the first assault but was soon rocking his head, grinding his hips and moaning loudly as Brett got into his rhythm.

Pumping like a piston, Brett's aching cock rammed Chuck's butt with a mind of its own. Racing headlong to a climax, it went crazy each time the skin stretched tight along its length and gave yet another sharp tug to the circumcised knob spearheading the assault. It was a hot plunger on its way to an atomic detonation, with all systems shouting, "Go!"

Boom! A fiery explosion went off in Brett's scrotum, searing his balls and sending gobs of hot semen rushing up his shaft. Crying out, he arched his spine for a second, then began a frenzied attack to satisfy his cock's insistent carnal craving for ass. Only by thrusting his cock right up Chuck's chute and leaving a gallon of cum behind would Brett be able to rest peaceful again.

"Yes! Yes! Yes!" screamed Chuck, feeling his insides going sticky with Brett's sizzling jism. "Fuck me! Fuck me! Fuck me!"

Brett threw his head back and let out a deep-throated moan as his volcanic-like eruption ran its full course.

Physically exhausted, his man-juice spent, Brett gingerly eased his still-hard cock out of the slick, steaming hole and collapsed onto Chuck's broad chest. He couldn't have been more content than at that moment, snuggling happy and secure against his sweat-drenched bed of sculpted muscle. It was all a dream, being with Chuck like that, a dream come true. He was in heaven.

Wrapping him in his strong arms, Chuck smiled and kissed Brett lightly on the lips. "'What more can I do to prove that you're the one I want? Anything. Name it."

"Just hold me," whispered Brett.

"I'll hold you forever," replied Chuck, grasping Brett even more tightly. "Now, get that Marty-crap out of your head. You're the only person I'm interested in."

Brett smiled back sheepishly. "I hear you."

"Good. I may be a little slow in showing it, but once I make up my mind I want something—or somebody—I never stop until I get it. I want you, Brett. In *and* out of the gym. I want you beside me when I win the Mr. America and I want to be the guy you come home to at night. Got that?"

"I got it, Chuck."

There was a deafening pause before Chuck quietly asked, "Well, how about it?"

Meeting the waiting eyes with his own, Brett smiled and said, "I think I'm going to like living with a future Mr. America."

Chuck broke into a broad grin and treated Brett to a bone-crushing bearhug. "I was hoping you'd say that! What say we get cleaned up and head over to my place? We can work on my posing for a while. I've got a few positions I think you might find very interesting."

Workout

THE GUYS ON State University's Bodybuilding Team were a rabid pack of intense, muscle-crazed animals. Fueled by a high-grade mixture of explosive adrenaline and super-charged testosterone, the macho muscle fanatics were a volatile group dedicated to radical routines, peak performance and the pursuit of the Perfect Pump.

Well on their way to attaining the ultimate in masculine musculature, they were committed, aggressive and egotistical competitors who could be cheerful, accommodating companions one minute and intimidating, dangerous assholes the next. It seemed the only one who could exert any sort of control over them other than the coach was Pete. It was a tough job but, as Pete so often quipped, somebody had to do it.

It was a tough job made even more demanding because their surging hormones had turned the hot, humpy, mega-muscular young men into a formidable bunch of walking hard-ons. With their near-insatiable libidos, the guys were constantly on the lookout for a good time. And after months of close physical and emotional contact with little or no privacy, they had been stripped of their hang-ups and inhibitions to the point where, within the group, a good time meant anything was possible. Sex was sex. All the better if it was done with a buddy. Better still if it was done with Pete.

And Pete? Pete was more than just a trainer who taped bum knees and picked up towels. He was everything from big brother and mother hen to best friend, confidant and fuckbuddy. It was a demanding, 24-hour job which at times could be frustrating, nerve-wracking and a real pain in the butt (figuratively and not-so figuratively speaking). But then, it also provided a lot of opportunities for personal satisfaction, instant gratification and some serious male bonding.

"Male bonding," mused Pete. "Let's hear it for Male Bonding." Fact was, Pete was "Male Bonding" with every guy on the squad at least once a week. Most of the action was pretty basic, tended to be one-sided (i.e. Pete did most of the work) and was usually all over with in less than fifteen minutes. But it was action nonetheless.

The use of Pete's special talents began one day after practice when he happened upon Hector Gonzalez jacking off in the showers. After a moment of awkward silence (Hector was embarrassed but too revved to stop), Pete threw caution to the wind and boldly walked over, dropped to his knees and gave the hunky Latino musclestud a serious blowjob. Despite mutual assurances of silence, word slowly got out among the guys and Pete's life was never the same again.

They all wanted a piece of him. Morning, noon and fucking night. Pete never thought he'd get tired of sex but, he had to admit, the team's Action on Demand attitude was beginning to wear him out. Their last home workout before flying to the big Mr. Collegiate Bodybuilding Contest had been the all-time capper, the ultimate in performance sexmusclekink. It started in the morning innocently enough but quickly got way, way out of hand.

With the coach off doing fuck-knows-what, Pete had been left alone in the gym with the fifteen boisterous young bucks thinking he'd be supervising a serious weight workout. The workout was serious, alright, in more ways than one.

With a radio blasting away in the background, the humpy musclestuds, clad only in jockstraps and sneakers (team rule: "You work it, you show it!"), swaggered through their usual gut-busting routines, maxing-out on poundages and reps, powering their way to "The Pump." If there was one thing these guys got off on it was a harsh, vein-popping, all-over pump. But, as usual, they had more than pumped muscles on their minds.

Between sets, things got testy as they all vied for Pete's attention and favor. Since Pete could help only one at a time the atmosphere in the weight room got real tense, real fast. No tactic was too obvious, no trick too cheap, no maneuver (short of clenched fists) too aggressive, low-down or dirty. Not if it meant an aching erection, cum-bloated balls or twitching asshole would be serviced by the best friend and trainer a horny young bodybuilder ever had. Fuck, the guys practically stood in line with a number, they were so eager for a turn.

Lawrence Talbot wanted a spotter so he could blast his pecs on the bench press. At 6′2″, with 250-pounds of massive, gym-tortured muscle and an intense, take-no-shit attitude, he got what he wanted. Talbot's idea of a spot meant Pete straddled him on the bench and took his latexed fuckpole up the ass while he did the exercise. Pete would match him stroke for stroke until either muscle failure kept the bar on Talbot's chest or Talbot's churning balls got the better of him and he blew more than his concentration. An interesting variation, and not for the faint of heart.

This time around, the scowling black heavyweight with the shaved head and sweat-drenched body managed to squeeze off a staggering 26 reps with 225 pounds on the bar (light for him) before the hot hole clamped around his throbbing dick detonated his jizz-laden balls. Barely racking the weight in time, he mashed Pete down on his erupting cock and emptied the contents of his fiery balls in an awesome display of brute force and sexual power. Mount St. Helens had nothing on this stud. Once his dick was satisfied, he politely thanked Pete for his assistance, checked his pecs in the mirror, then casually went on to his next exercise like nothing out of the ordinary had happened. Then again, Pete had to admit, the guy was right.

Alan Takahashi got off on squats, lots of them, and he had the huge tree-trunk thighs to prove it. That morning he used 400 pounds on the bar to blitz his legs into total submission, then called Pete over on the pretext his quads were cramping. Once the 5′10″, 190-pound black-haired weight warrior had Pete kneeling in front of him deep-massaging his enormous power-packed thighs (no easy task, considering how pumped they were), he hauled out his hard, cum-dripping cock and smugly asked, "How about working on this for a while instead?" Pete grinned, popped the short but amazingly thick hunk of meat in his mouth and went to work. Primed as he was, it didn't take long before Takahashi shot his load and happily trotted off.

Nick Angelopoulos possessed a naive, boyish charm but he was no dummy. Not when it came to getting what he wanted. He knew Pete always watched him when he did his leg curls because lying face down on the inverted V-shaped padded bench not only forced his olive-hued bubblebutt high into the air but each torturous contraction caused the magnificent curved globes to solidify into mouth-watering twin peaks of hard, striated muscle. And he knew how much Pete got off on striated twin peaks.

Set finished, Angelopoulos eased off the bench all hot and sweaty and made an elaborate show of stretching out his pumped legs and rubbing his aching ass. More for Pete's benefit than his own, to be sure. Suddenly furrowing his brow, he strolled over and in that hesitant, wide-eyed innocent voice of his, that never failed to sucker-punch Pete, asked, "You don't, you know, think my glutes are, maybe, getting too big, do you?" Then he turned and presented his glistening ass for Pete's inspection, slowly grinding his hips to show it from various angles, tensing it a couple of times to illustrate the difference between flexed and relaxed, and bending over to grab his ankles so he could display it in a moon pose.

Pete gave a little whimper and his hard cock surged to epic, painful proportions. Sliding a hand over the dazzling, satin-smooth buttcheeks he swallowed the lump in his throat and mumbled, "No, I think they're just about perfect." His center finger found the puckered rosebud, circled the inviting pink portal a few times before it gently popped the seal and disappeared inside.

Now it was Angelopoulos who whimpered. And groaned. Primed by the leg curls, the finger fucking drove him crazy. Pulling Pete along with his ass, he hobbled over to where he could lean against a rack of dumbbells and moaned, "Fuck me, Pete. Right here, right now."

So, knowing it was what they both wanted, Pete slipped on a rubber and in front of everyone fucked the living shit out of the most beautiful ass on the team. Not bad work if you can get it, he mused.

Having decided long ago that he didn't have the physical ingredients to beat more genetically-gifted bodybuilders, Kevin "Kornhole" Kornder was obsessed with packing on as much size, shape and mass as possible in his quest for muscle fame and notoriety. A strikingly handsome senior with a bad case of acne, he stood only 5′3″ in height but weighed an astounding 230 pounds—all of it monstrous, mind-boggling muscle. He was massive to the point of being grotesque, "freaky" even by hard-core gym standards and as close to fitting the term "musclebound" as a guy could get. He had yet to win a contest but he loved the way his body grossed-out the public and mind-fucked the competition.

He also loved getting his ass eaten out. Yup, liked nothing better than a good, slurpy, vigorous rimming. He powered through his workout as usual then, finally catching Pete's eye, motioned he wanted to work his calves. Donkey calf raises, Kornder-style. Fine by Pete.

Bent over an exercise bench with the balls of his feet on a thick block of wood and Takahashi astride his hips for added weight, Kornder went up and down on his toes in slow motion brutalizing his huge, tear-drop shaped calves. Behind him, struggling to keep the rock-hard cheeks of the over-developed bubblebutt apart with his hands while he buried his nose in the smooth hairless crack and worked the luscious pink shithole with his tongue, knelt Pete.

Top of his class in Rimming 101, Pete drove Kornder fucking crazy with his expert asshole ministrations. His tongue licked, lapped, slurped, dabbed and tickled the twitching rosebud, alternating between light, lingering, gentle caresses and bold, forceful jabs. Once in a while, for a wicked change of pace, he'd rake his teeth over the puckered hole or push his tongue all the way in and really clean Kornder's clock.

His calf workout all but forgotten, Kornder bucked and squirmed under Pete's concerted tongue lashing, his stubby little cock tenting his jockstrap, his head rolling about in unbridled delight. He swore a solid blue streak under his breath the whole time until he let out a choked, "Oh, fuck me all to hell, baby," grabbed his cock and pounded his pud into a sticky submission. A load lighter, he thanked Pete and Takahashi for their help, then lumbered over to a mirror to gloat over his pumped calves.

Subtlety was not a word in Frank Borrelli's vocabulary. The strutting middle-weight contender waited until the end of his workout so that his muscle-packed, super-defined body was pumped to its max and then called Pete over to watch his posing routine. He punched out one incredible pose after another. Front double biceps. Side chest. Rear lat spread. Moon pose. Most muscular. Legs and abs. He hit them all, most of them twice, as much for his own egotistical benefit and smug satisfaction as Pete's admiring, lustful perusal.

Then, claiming it was too tight and getting in the way, he yanked off his jockstrap and after making a big production of scratching his nuts and stroking his meat proceeded to do his whole routine again. Between the erect, horse-sized dick swinging between his rippling legs and his pumped, corded muscles, it was a wonder any blood at all was getting to his head. There must have been enough, though, because without taking his eyes off himself in the mirror he gasped out between poses, "Pete, I'm almost there. You gotta . . . help me!..

"You mean," Pete smirked, "do that fag thing?"

Borrelli's eyes met Pete's and he smirked back, "Yeh, that fag thing."

So without further hesitation, Pete dropped to his knees and gave the musclestud what he wanted: a major, vein-popping blowjob. Borrelli kept throwing one pose after another the whole time, losing himself in the sex'n'flex muscletrip right up until the last possible moment. He held out one last split second hoping to achieve the maximum in mind-blowing, body-shattering momentum, then crabbed into a most-muscular at exactly the same instant his nuts detonated, blowing himself straight to kingdom cum. By the time he was through flexing and spewing sperm, his sack was hanging low and empty and his exhausted muscles were sagging as limp as his dangling dick. The satisfied look on his face, however, showed he had got what he wanted.

Jack O'Reilly also waited until the end of his workout. Despite the obvious (5′11″, 210-pounds of awesome, mind-blowing muscle), the unrelenting "no pain, no gain" philosophy of the weight room sometimes did a number on the auburn-haired hunk and he got it into his head that he didn't hurt enough to call himself a competitive bodybuilder. It was irrational, he knew, but it wasn't until Pete came along that he had an understanding friend who would help him undergo the penance necessary to atone for his "laziness."

At the lat pulldown machine, where he first stripped the stud's rank, sweat-sodden, piss-stained jockstrap from his bulging crotch and wrapped it mask-like over the man's nose and mouth, Pete fitted the Instruments of Atonement: a leather cockring and ball harness, tit clamps and a large butt plug. Then, once O'Reilly had his massive thighs wedged under the padded restraining bar to hold his body in place and was cranking off wide-grip lat pulldowns against 180 pounds worth of iron resistance, Pete brought out the riding crop.

With practiced precision, he laid stroke after wicked stroke across O'Reilly's shoulders, back, thighs, abs and chest—any place he could land a good, clean shot—at the same time barking at the musclestud to "Squeeze it, Feel the burn, Pump it," and "Watch your form!"

In an amazing display of concentration and fortitude, O'Reilly absorbed the punishment and channelled the pain to focus even more intently on his quest. He performed set after strict, agonizing set, all the while gasping out a monotonal chant of his own: "More! Again! Harder! I gotta feel it! No pain, no gain!"

He steamrollered through an incredible number of repetitions until his tormented psyche finally propelled his exhausted body past its normal pain threshold and thrust it into the rarified strata of ultra-intense, muscle and mind-expanding superpain most hardcore bodybuilders only dream of achieving. Gasping out a tortured "Yesss!" O'Reilly hit nirvana and his cock exploded in a violent release of thick, creamy cum to celebrate. Hanging onto the lat pulldown bar for dear life, he jerked and spasmed uncontrollably while his orgasm ran its full, staggering course in an awesome display of solomusclesex pyrotechnics.

It shook O'Reilly to the very core of his being but the orgasm somehow did the trick. When it was over the young musclestud was totally drained but calm and contented. His demons were exorcised and he'd be okay again. For a while.

Before the team split for lunch Pete called them over for one last rah-rah, one-from-the-heart pep-talk. He told them how awesome they were physically, how mind-blowing they were on the posing platform, and how fucking proud he was of each and every one of them. He half expected his impromptu little speech to be met with mock embarrassment at the very least or, at the worst, open scorn and derision. But to his surprise and satisfaction they met his sincerity with an honest and emotional outpouring of their own.

They shouted, stomped, hooted, hollered and high-fived, all with big shit-eatin' grins on their faces and their chests bursting with pride. When Pete finished they all squeezed in tight for an intense group hug. Basic, primal and totally spontaneous, it demonstrated just how far they had come together. They stayed like that —hard sweaty muscular flesh happily pressed against more hard sweaty muscular flesh—until just when Pete thought it couldn't possibly get any better they formed a tight circle around him and boldly beat their impressive collection of rigid, mouth-watering meat with a single thought in mind: to show him their unabashed respect, admiration and devotion in the most personal way they knew how. Fifteen proud macho young musclestuds paid Pete tribute by drenching him with their ultimate masculine essence.

It was beautiful, absolutely fucking beautiful, and the gesture wasn't lost on Pete. Emotionally choked long after the guys were whooping it up in the showers, he just stood there, covered in cum, thinking that the fuckers were the best friends a man could ever hope to have.

By the time Pete finally hit the showers himself there was only one towel left hanging on the railing. He smiled, wondering who it belonged to, and stepped inside. With all the showers still going full blast, the accumulated heat and swirling mist had turned the room into a veritable steambath. The vapor was so thick Pete could barely see his hand in front of his face. But the surreal, erotic atmosphere just made finding Hector Gonzalez all the more rewarding. Gonzalez grinned seductively and Pete went weak at the knees. Yup, the best for last.

The guy was a knockout. A humpy bodybuilder who had it all: size, symmetry, awesome definition, devastating good looks, mega-watt charisma, animal sex appeal, stamina and a cock that could choke a horse. "You're just in time," he said.

"For what?" asked Pete.

"To shave me," Gonzalez replied, a mischievous twinkle in his eye. "For the contest."

"Oh, right." Now it was Pete's turn to grin. Except for his head and armpits, the only hair on Gonzalez' body was a small patch at his crotch. But the pretense of the shave allowed Pete the opportunity to lather up every square inch of the humpy 5′6″, 145-pound Latino and in doing so get his hands on some spectacular, near-perfect musculature in the process.

Gonzalez loved getting the lather/massage almost as much as Pete loved giving it to him. He loved having his hard-won physical attributes worshipped and adored by someone he himself respected. He loved the feel of strong fingers marvelling at his wide shoulders, broad back, bulging arms, squared pecs, wasp waist, washboard abs, striated ass, rippling thighs and tear-drop calves. He loved being able to cut all the pretentious games and shit in his life and enter into an uncomplicated world of total male pleasure. And most of all, he loved it when Pete finally, *finally*, wrapped his lips around the head of his engorged manmeat and slowly, gently, with infinite care and tenderness, swallowed every one of his thick, throbbing eight inches and showed him what an experienced, expert cocksucker could do.

Pete pulled the long, rubbery foreskin back and slid his tongue around and around the huge, helmet-shaped cockhead. He kept that up until Gonzalez started moaning and groaning and then, in one smooth move, sucked the whole bloated shaft into his mouth and played it for all he was worth. In no time Gonzalez was leaning on him for support and swearing softly in Spanish. When, that is, he wasn't gasping for breath.

Gonzalez had a lot of endurance but even he couldn't withstand Pete's withering assault and expertise forever. Unable to hold back the fiery juices churned up in his mahogany-hued balls a moment longer, with a choked sob and a loud groan he gave a mighty shudder and—*bam!*—started spraying cum faster than an Uzi spits bullets.

Bam! Bam! Bam! Gonzalez bucked harder than a rodeo bronc rider as he cut loose with his luscious Latin elixir. The intensity of his orgasm was spectacular and forced Pete to swallow like crazy if he wasn't going to drown in a sea of cum.

Once the fireworks were over came the part Pete liked best. Gonzalez became surprisingly affectionate. The hot-blooded mini-volcano loved to hold and be held and could cuddle quite contentedly for what seemed like hours. He also loved to kiss. It didn't seem to matter that Pete was a guy (or maybe that was the reason) because he returned the long, slow, deep kisses Pete served up with an ardor and passion all his own.

It was getting scarey. While the macho superstud never talked about his feelings, Pete sensed that maybe, just maybe, Gonzalez had the same kind of feelings for him that he had for Gonzalez. Feelings that were getting beyond the buddy-buddy. Pete worked hard at keeping a lid on his emotions but, deep down, he had to admit it was a losing battle. He liked Gonzalez. He liked him a lot.

The shave, when they finally got around to it, took all of thirty seconds. The hard part was keeping Gonzalez' excited cock out of harm's way. Then, laughing arm in arm like a couple of schoolboys, the two gymjocks stumbled into the locker room where—"Oh, shit"—they found Coach waiting for them. A scowling, fuming, totally pissed-off Coach.

"Well, ain't this just too fucking cozy," snarled the 5′10″, 198-pound blond behemoth.

Quickly disentangling himself, Pete slapped Gonzalez on the ass and mumbled, "I'll catch you later."

Gonzalez gave a nervous wink and retorted, "I sure hope so dude. Later."

The tension was so thick while Coach waited for Gonzalez to clear out that Pete could have cut it with a knife. From the look on Coach's face there was no way he was going to get out of this unscathed. Punishment was inescapable.

If he hadn't been shitting bricks about what was going to happen next, Pete might have actually enjoyed the sight in front of him a whole lot more. God knows, it was a sight that usually brought a lump to his jockstrap. Coach hadn't competed in over ten years but genetics and regular heavy-duty workouts still kept him in prime condition. In his white tanktop and baggy black sweatpants he was a muscle fantasy knockout.

Alone at last, Coach walked up to Pete and growled, "Don't think I don't know what the fuck's been going on between you and the team."

Pete swallowed hard. He didn't know which scared him most: the fear of Coach's wrath and retribution or his insane desire to latch onto the hot man's honkin' big nipples and haul him in close for some serious lip-lock. "Sir?"

"Pete, you are one hell of a trainer, but I can no longer ignore the fact that you are also the team's resident muscle-loving cocksucking asslicking tit-twisting ball-punching sex maniac."

"Uh . . . Yes, Sir. I guess I am."

"Okay. So what I want to know is: how the fuck do I get in on one of your special workouts?"

"What—?" Pete heaved a deep sigh when it sunk in that Coach

was totally serious. “Gee, Coach, all you gotta do is ask,” he chided.

“Well, hell,” snorted Coach, “I’m asking. I’m asking big time!” He yanked down his sweatpants and jock and brandished an impressive nine-inch uncut cum-dripping boner.

“Whoa, you certainly are,” Pete agreed. Licking his lips, he dropped to his knees and cheerfully announced, “One Special Workout coming up!”

Stripped for Action

GEORGE KROMIDAS STEPPED OUT of the showers and padded gingerly across the locker room to where Brad was waiting. He was soaked. Drenched. His heavy coat of thick black body hair was plastered to his olive skin like fur on a wet sea otter, sensuously accenting all the peaks, valleys and chiseled edges of his hard, muscled body.

The dense mat was everywhere. Every-fucking-where! Some parts—forearms, legs, pecs, armpits, the center strip of his stomach, the small of his back to the crack of his ass, his pubic patch—were more lush and overgrown than others but there wasn't a single area without some hair growing from it. Even his toes had little tufts sprouting from them.

"You ever shave anyone before?" he asked, nervously eyeing all the accoutrements of his pending ordeal spread out on a nearby bench. "I mean . . . all over?"

"I've got a couple of buddies who are serious bodybuilders. I'm always shaving them for contests," Brad replied. He reached over and squeezed a brawny shoulder. "Hey, relax, it won't hurt a bit. You might even get to like it."

Brad knew he was going to like it. He'd dreamed of getting his hands on the 5′8″, 170-pound wrestler ever since the guy showed up at try-outs. He sensed a mutual attraction but it wasn't until late that very afternoon when the opportunity to find out presented itself. Ironically, it was the coach who provided the opportunity.

It had been a particularly grueling workout and, as usual, Kromidas bore the brunt of the coach's post-practice tirade. Brad's heart went out to the depressed grappler and he found himself wishing he could gather the humpy 170-pounder in his arms and shield him from the coach's wrath. He was thinking that once he had the furry hunk in his arms he could soothe his bruised and battered ego by whispering soft words of encouragement in his ear while running his fingers through the thick mat of luxurious black hair covering the stud's magnificent body. He was thinking that from there it'd be oh-so-simple to run his hands down to that perfect ass and pry those breath-taking, curved buttcheeks apart and slip his aching cock up that pretty pink shitchute and give him the fuck of his ever-loving life.

Brad was thinking, "Yeah, I'll get my hands on him—when hell freezes over," when the coach suddenly bellowed, "It's all that hair, Kromidas. That hair all over your body. It makes you look like a man. You see, on my team only men have hair on their body so I just naturally assumed. . . . But hey, that's okay, I got things figured out now. I ain't going to mistake you for a man again. If you're going to wrestle like a baby and cry like a baby then you're damn-well going to look like a baby! Brad—yeah, I'm talking to you!—shave him! You heard me, shave every last hair off Kromidas' body. Chest, back, legs, ass, pubes, head, even his goddamn eyebrows. I want Kromidas smooth as a baby's butt by tomorrow's practice. And you're to keep shaving him until I decide he's wrestling like a man. When he wrestles like a man, he can have hair like a man."

Brad looked at the dripping wet hunk and thought, "A baby he's not." He gave the shoulder another squeeze and said, "Let's do the easy stuff first."

Using a little foam, a safety razor and a technique honed over dozens of shaves, Brad quickly stripped Kromidas' hands, arms, shoulders and back of its pelt. A series of well-executed strokes turned the man into an arresting study in contrasts: a clash of smooth bare skin and thick black hair.

The head next. From the back, up over the sides and crown and down to the forehead, the flashing blade made short shrift of the trendy, salon-styled mane. Not even in Marine boot camp had a scalp ever been so closely or completely shorn. A couple of strokes and the eyebrows were gone, too.

Brad stepped back to admire his handiwork. To his credit, there wasn't a knick or leftover stubble anywhere on the man's head. It was as clean and smooth as a grunt's helmet. And twice as sexy.

Sensing a momentary respite, Kromidas hesitantly reached up for a feel. "How's it—oh, fuck." He stood and peered into a nearby mirror. "Oh, fuck . . . I look like a geek." Tears welled in his eyes. "Coach hates me, he really hates my guts.'

"He doesn't hate you," admonished Brad. "This is his way of

motivating you, of making you work harder."

"By humiliating me? By turning me into a geek?"

Brad grabbed Kromidas by the shoulders and growled in his face, "Who says you look like a geek? With or without hair you're a fucking hot man. And the only way you can be humiliated is if you yourself allow it. Remember that!"

"Yes, Sir."

"Okay. Now hit the showers. Wash off that crap and then we'll start on your chest."

Two minutes later Kromidas was once again standing dripping wet in front of Brad. He was still glum but his anger and humiliation were tempered now with a sense of gritty defiance. Taking a deep breath, he looked Brad right in the eye and pointedly asked, "Do you really think I'm a fucking hot man?"

Brad's heart leapt to his mouth but he managed to maintain eye contact. "Yes, I really do."

"Good. I think you're hot, too." He thrust out his chest and said, "Let's do it."

Applying the foam gave Brad the chance to finally get his hands on the wide expanse of Kromidas' sculpted pecs. No doubt about it, they were masterpieces of male musculature.

"I, uh . . . like working my chest," murmured Kromidas. It came out more like an apology than a statement of fact.

"No shit," snorted Brad. He grinned at the embarrassed stud and playfully grabbed a handful of left pec. "Keep up the good work. The bigger and harder, the better."

Kromidas relaxed and shyly grinned back. Then, in a surprisingly bold move for him, he suddenly flexed so that the pec under Brad's hand contracted into a thick, solid slab of bulging, molded muscle. "Hard enough for you?"

Brad gave the peaked mound an extensive tactile examination and proclaimed, "Sure impresses me all to hell!"

The pec wasn't the only part of Kromidas' anatomy to solidify. The hunk's stubby uncut dick had turned into a decent 7-inch, fat-as-a-beer-can, tantalizing piece of manmeat with a foreskin so long it still covered most of the plump, rounded cockhead.

Brad was tempted, mighty tempted, to make a grab for the thick piledriver, knowing that was what Kromidas wanted him to do. But it's always more interesting to keep a suitor off-balance, he thought, and besides, he truly wanted to spend as much time as possible with the hot and humpy man. Still, he had to admit it was time for a change of tack. A radical change of tack.

He hurriedly finished coating the chest and abs with foam (it was a kick, no other way to describe it, how the stud sucked in his breath when he got down to the edges of his pubic patch) and then, before Kromidas really knew what he was doing, wiped the foam from the two baby-soft, quarter-sized nipples and gave them a good hard pinch.

"Oww! What the heck was that for?"

"To get your nipples hard. Now they'll pop right up and I'll be able to spot them without any trouble. Wouldn't want me to accidentally slice them off, would you?"

This was something Kromidas hadn't considered. "No," he mumbled, clearly imagining the worst. His naiveté was disarming.

"I thought not. See? What'd I tell you? All nice and big and hard. Couldn't miss these babies now. Still, you know, maybe I'd better do it again. Just to be on the safe side." Brad knew he was pushing his luck. He fully expected Kromidas to put a stop to his blatant sexploitation.

But the good-looking grappler didn't say a word. Not when Brad took the puckered, dark brown rosettes in his fingertips, squeezed them, and kept on squeezing them. Not when he tightened his grip and slowly rotated the tits back and forth like radio dials. Not even when he dug his thumbnails into the tender, virgin flesh and caused what must have been excruciating pain to a tit novice like Kromidas (of course, it is difficult to say anything through tightly clenched teeth). Nope, not a word.

Brad released the tortured tits and nodded in appreciation. Good, very good. He noted, too, that the foreskin on Kromidas' bloated, throbbing cock was fully retracted now and a large drop of pre-cum had formed at the pisshole. Even better. This kid would go far. He smiled slightly, brushed the backs of his fingers against the perky red nips (nice how Kromidas winced) and said matter-of-factly, "Sure won't miss these babies now."

"No, I guess not. Thanks, Brad."

"My pleasure." Satisfied, Brad picked up the razor and went back to work.

The size and hardness of the broad, sweeping chest would have made shaving relatively easy if it weren't for the incredible density of the thick hair growing on it. It was like hacking through jungle. Instead of a few long strokes Brad was forced to use a series of short, choppy ones. Instead of mowing great swaths he had to scrape away at the coat in small sections. It wasn't particularly difficult but, fuck, it was time consuming.

Not that Brad was complaining. By slowing down and concentrating on what he was doing he heightened the tension and prolonged the experience. It was a real turn-on to slowly strip away a proud adult male's proof of manhood and leave him with smooth, boyish skin. Even better when the stripping away revealed an ultra-defined body of Herculean proportions.

There was something else, too. Something which Brad always found made any shaving scene a compelling exercise in eroticism. It doesn't matter how strong and confident a hairy man is, remove his fur, his outward badge of masculinity, and he is left exposed, vulnerable and malleable. Physically and mentally. Just as Kromidas was now.

"How ya doing?" Brad asked, drawing the flat of his hand lightly across the magnificent bare chest and abs.

"I'm okay," whimpered Kromidas.

Bullshit. He was a cocked pistol with a hair trigger. His whimper down-geared to a deep moan when Brad continued lower and wrapped his fingers tightly around the thick piledriver. "Now comes the fun part," Brad smirked, giving the dick a squeeze.

As long as Kromidas stayed relaxed, shaving the bulk of his legs was relatively easy. Because of their beefy dimensions, each pull of the razor sliced a good-sized strip of hair and foam from the furry hindquarters. It was only when he choked, when the stress got to him and he tensed, causing his thighs and calves to bunch into tightly-wound cables that shaving became difficult. All the peaks, valleys, curves and sharp edges made a clean sweep virtually impossible and half the battle became just getting the stud to ease up. Not a bad job, either, considering it meant a certain amount of leg massage and butch "Hey, relax, man" buddy-talk.

By the time Brad got up off his knees the only hair Kromidas had left on his humpy, muscular body was on his ass, at his groin, and in a thin strip between his legs joining the two. It was almost as if he were wearing a tiny bikini brief, except the "fabric" of this model did nothing to hide his privates.

"Bend over and spread your legs." The words almost caught in Brad's throat. "Wider. Yeah, lean on the bench for support. Wider. Yeah, that's it. I wanna see your crack split wide open."

"Like this, Sir?"

"Perfect." Deliberately gripping one of the hairy buttcheeks so that his thumb rested on the puckered pink asshole, Brad went to work on the upturned bubblebutt. The tight little buns were so smooth and hard, their texture as soft and lustrous as satin with not a mark or blemish to mar their surface, that they were, without a doubt, the epitome of Grade-A prime ass. A joy to shave, they were nothing short of gut-wrenching to touch. Absolutely gut-wrenching.

And the more Brad fussed with the razor, cutting away more and more of the curly black fleece, the less subtle he became massaging the puckered orifice. He kept up the pressure (breaking only to suck his thumb to get it wet) until, at about the same time he got the last of the butthair, Kromidas let out a moan, his hole relaxed, and Brad's thumb slid all the way in. "Atta boy."

Wasting no time, Brad went right to work doing a thumbfucking number on the beautiful splayed ass before him. Between jabbing in and out, twisting back and forth, and ricocheting around the rim of the sensitive sphincter, it wasn't long before he had Kromidas in the throes of Ass Heaven. Deliberately waiting until the stud was mere seconds away from blowing his wad he suddenly pulled out, gave the tensed ass a hard slap and ordered, "Up on the bench, facing me, kiddo. Time for your short and curlies."

Kromidas was so revved and close to coming, the abrupt pullout damn-near sent him into a convulsive tailspin. It took a lot of effort and will-power to pull himself together, haul his quivering ass up onto the bench and stand tall. "Ready, Sir," he panted. Yeh, he was ready, alright.

"Spoken like a man." Holding onto Kromidas' thick, fat prick to keep it out of harm's way, Brad went to work on the dense black bush at the man's groin. All the while the shining blade went scrape, scrape, scrape and gobs of foam and black hair were landing splat, splat, splat he kept pounding away on the throbbing pud. It was great how the thick foreskin slid back and forth along the pulsing rod, bunching up at the base to expose the fat, glistening cockhead and then sliding back over the end of it.

Brad could have kept pumping away like that for hours if he didn't have more to keep him busy. "Here, hold your cock up out of the way, Kromidas," he said.

"Ah, er . . . Excuse me, Sir, but what are you doing?"

Brad looked up and quite innocently asked, "What does it look like I'm doing?"

"Well, Sir, it . . . uh, looks like you're holding my balls, Sir."

"Right again, Kromidas. Coach said to shave everything so that's what I'm doing. Geez, Kromidas, you've got the hairiest damn balls I've ever seen." Brad collared the sac so the nuts bunched together tight at the bottom and started in with the razor. "Yup, real hairy."

"I'm sorry, Brad." Kromidas swallowed hard as the blade slid over his bulging pouch.

"Nothing to apologize for, stud. Why, I'm a big fan of hairy balls. It's a real shame you're going to lose yours. The hair, that is, not the balls. But then (and here Brad winked up at the rigid man), I'm a big fan of smooth balls, too."

"That's, ah, nice to know."

"Steady, Kromidas. Steady."

Once the sizable nutsac was clean as a whistle and smooth as silk, Brad tugged and twisted it a couple of times (pleased how Kromidas silently accepted the treatment) and said, "Not bad, stud, if I do say so myself. Don't worry, we're almost finished. Only one place left. Right between your legs. Best way to do it is for you to lie on your back and lift your legs up."

Kromidas was long past questioning orders. On his back, his legs to his chest, he offered his puckered pink hole in a clear act of submission and raging desire. He wanted to be exposed and wide open. He wanted to be fucked, wanted it bad. And he wanted it from Brad.

"There. All finished." Brad set the razor down and admired both his handiwork and his "canvas." His cock throbbed in wanton anticipation as his eyes devoured the pretty pink asshole and pulsing cum-dripping cock, feasted on the dense musculature rippling under the smooth, freshly-shorn skin, marvelled at the handsome face and striking bare head, and fell for the pleading puppydog eyes looking up at him. The man was a knock-out, an absolute fucking knock-out.

"Fuck me, Sir," begged Kromidas. "I've been dreaming of having your cock in me for a long time. Please don't make me wait for it any longer. I want it, I want it bad. And I know you want to do it. So do it, Brad. Do it now. Fuck me. Fuck me hard and fuck me long! *Please*!"

Who could resist such an insistent invitation? Brad stripped off his gym shorts and jock, grabbed a condom and bottle of lube from his gym bag and knelt before Kromidas' wide-spread legs and hungry hole. He rolled on the latex, squeezed out some gel and eased into place. Kromidas was so hot to trot that all Brad needed was one short, concerted push and he slipped in all the way to his cum-laden nuts, damn-near tripping his own trigger in the process. "Holyfuckingeezus!" he gasped.

"Omigod! Oh fuck, that feels good," moaned Kromidas. "It feels incredible! Even better than I'd dreamed it would feel! Yeah, now do it, Brad. Give me your cock! Give me your big man's cock! Fuck me! Fuck the living daylights out of me!"

So Brad fucked him. And it was a great fuck, too. A really great, fucking wonderful fuck! Brad hit his stride early and became a wild, sex-crazed animal. His cock pounded Kromidas' super-tight shitchute in a dazzling, mind-blowing variety of heart-stopping, toe-curling strokes. One minute short and rapid-fire, the next, long and luxuriously drawn-out. Brad amazed even himself, it was so great. Absolutely fucking . . . "Ah! Ah!! Ahhhhhhhhhhh!"

Kromidas suddenly started bucking and thrashing around like a hog-tied heifer, going apeshit right out of control. His throbbing piledriver, without so much as a finger on it, started blasting out big cumwads so thick and fast they went *wap! wap! wap!* on his heaving chest. "Ah! Ah! Oh yes, Sir! That's it! oh fuck, *That's it! Yessss!*"

Two seconds later—*bam!*—the hot ass clamped around Brad's dick pushed him right over the edge. A monumental explosion went off in his nuts and he lost it, totally lost it, in one of the hardest, most intense orgasms of his whole life. It didn't let up until every last drop of cum had been squeezed from his balls and he'd been left drained, exhausted and utterly spent. "Ahhhhhhhh. . . ."

Awash in the afterglow of their first fuck, Kromidas pulled Brad tight against him as they bearhugged on the locker room floor. He heaved a deep sigh of relief and said dreamily, "You're right. I could really get to like this shaving thing. I could get to like it so much I might never have hair again."

"No complaints from me on that score," replied Brad, running an appreciative hand over the broad slabs of smooth pec-muscle rising and falling next to him. "It's gonna be a pleasure keeping you stripped and ready for action."

"Mmmm, let's hear it for action," Kromidas murmured, just before giving Brad a long, lingering, passion-filled kiss. When he finally came up for air he grinned mischievously and added, "Who knows, it might even help my wrestling."

Most Muscular

TEN THIRTY AT NIGHT, and the gym was still as hot and humid as a sauna! The odor of mansweat and unwashed jockstraps hung in the air. The place reeked of strutting machismo and ultra-masculinity. Anything could happen in a place like this, and just thinking about the possibilities made Dean hot and horny.

He set the seventy-pound dumb-bells down on their rack and felt the blood flooding into his biceps, which throbbed in that gut-wrenching, masochistic kind of pain that comes from exerting the body past its normal limits. Turning to a mirror, he whipped off his T-shirt and hit a double biceps pose. "Not bad. Not fucking bad."

At twenty-three, Dean stood 5′9″ and weighed a solid 180 pounds. Although not tall, he had sleek lines and razor-sharp definition. What with his impressive physique, his blond, blue-eyed, all-American good looks, and the thick slab of meat he packed in his jockstrap, he was definitely hot stuff. And he knew it. Trouble was, he couldn't get Mike Gates to know it!

Big Mike Gates, holder of umpteen bodybuilding titles, was about forty-five years old, stood 5′8″ tall, weighed somewhere in the neighborhood of 200 pounds, and was built like a brick shit-house. He'd been bodybuilding for close to thirty years and had the muscles to show for it. In addition to his Herculean physique, he had dark, piercing eyes, a tanned and weather-beaten complexion, closely-cropped black hair, and a heavy basket. The sum of these impressive parts was pure, animal sex appeal. But Mike was a loner who never mixed with the other guys in the gym. He barely said two words in the course of a workout, even to his training partner. And he drove Dean up the wall.

That asshole. That fucking prima donna! Dean thought when he spied his prey at the bench press whipping through a fast eight reps. Mike was alone, as usual. In fact, the two of them were the only ones left in the place. Dean swaggered over, took one look at the sweat-drenched muscle-stud lying on the bench, and got a raging hard-on.

Mike rose to a sitting position and froze when he found Dean glaring at him. The older man ran a hand over his pecs as he silently gave Dean the once-over. Dean's erection was clearly visible through his jock and gym shorts.

"Three hundred pounds?" sneered Dean. "Is that all? You ain't going to keep those big, award-winning muscles if you dick around with only three hundred pounds. You better do another set before you deflate. Come on, old man, let's see you do another set."

Mike fixed Dean with a steady, dispassionate gaze. Then, with a slight smile, he slid under the bar and eased off another eight reps. Unfazed, he stood up, motioned towards the weight, and growled, "Your turn."

Defiantly, Dean lay down on the bench and hefted the bar over his chest. The first four reps were easy, a piece of cake. The fatigue started during the fifth rep, a real pain arrived during the sixth, and the terrifying realization that he had bitten off more than he could chew hit him as he struggled to finish the seventh.

One more rep. The weight-laden bar lowered to his chest, grazed his nipples and . . . stayed there. There was no way, no fucking way he was going to get the bar up again! His arms shook, his veins bulged, and sweat poured off him in rivers. Panic twisted his gut into a million knots. "Oh, God," he groaned, "I can't do it. Help me, Mike. Help me!"

Stripping off his shorts and his jockstrap, Mike straddled Dean's waist and waved his hard cock at him. "If you want this man's meat—and I think you do—you'll finish that rep."

"Please, Mike!" pleaded Dean, "I can't do it!"

Mike's smile broadened. With a mouthful of spit to help ease him down the road, Mike began a long, slow love affair with his dick, slip-sliding the length of his thick seven inches close to Dean's pain-wracked face. "I think you can."

"You bastard!" Goaded by anger, frustration and unbridled lust, Dean pushed and strained with all his might until, finally, the weight was back on its stand. Not once had he taken his eyes off the throbbing head of Mike's mouth-watering cock. Trembling, Dean got to his feet.

"You okay?" Mike didn't sound too concerned, but at least he'd stopped beating his meat to ask. It was still hard, though, still fiery-red, and pre-cum oozed from the pisshole in tiny droplets.

"I'm okay," replied Dean weakly, feeling as though he'd just had the shit kicked out of him. In a way, he had.

"Good." Suddenly, storming like an enraged bull, Mike jabbed a finger under Dean's nose and roared, "Don't *ever* pull a stupid stunt like that again, you hear me? Show-offs only hurt themselves. Do it again and I'll whip your friggin' ass!"

The unexpected rebuke stung harder than a real slap. Feeling bad already, Dean found the outburst more than he could handle. "I won't, I promise." With his shame complete and absolute, he mumbled, "Sorry to bother you," then turned to leave. Mike caught his arm and their eyes locked.

"Lecture over," whispered Mike. Pulling Dean close, he gave him a tender kiss on the lips. "You bother me all right, kid. You bother me in the worst way."

Backing Dean against a mirrored wall, Mike pressed another long, passion-filled kiss on the younger man's hot, pliant lips while his hands roamed freely over the chiseled edges and hard, sharp curves of Dean's muscular body. One moment he fondled the bulge of Dean's straining biceps, the next the curve of his flexed pectorals and the sweep of his flared lats. Slipping his hands under Dean's gym shorts, Mike grabbed the muscular ass and gave it a hard, unrelenting massage until Dean's whimper warned him to take things easy, at least the first time around. "Mmmmm, I'm going to like fucking you."

Dean dropped to his knees in front of Mike's thick, seven-inch tool. "You said I could have it if I finished the rep," he said. When Mike nodded in reply, Dean pounced on the older man's hard meat and worked it over until he had Mike groaning with satisfaction.

"Oh, yeah, that's it, kid. Suck that cock. Suck my Mr. America meat. Suck it, fuckin' choke on it!" Mike grabbed the sides of Dean's head and started face-fucking him, ramming his hot seven inches down Dean's throat again and again and again, making Dean gag and choke and beg for more.

Suddenly, to Dean's amazement, Mike pulled out and hauled him to his feet. Then Mike went down on *him*, sucking for all he was worth, taking Dean's eight inches of uncut manmeat like it was the sweetest piece of candy in town. Dean thrashed around and rolled his head in sheer pleasure. "Oh fuck, yes!"

Just when Dean thought he might go over the brink, Mike stood up and gave him another long, inflamed kiss. Then Mike picked him up like a sack of potatoes and gently laid him on his back on the bench press. The next thing he knew, Dean's legs were over his head and Mike the muscle-stud was eating his ass as though it was the sweetest, best-tasting thing in town.

In no time, Dean was squirming under the attack, not daring to breathe, biting his tongue to keep quiet and feeling as though his cock would explode any second. It was throbbing so hard he was afraid to touch it. "God, Mike, stop! I can't take much more of this. I can't!"

"You can't, huh?" grinned Mike. "That's good to hear." He let Dean's feet back down on the floor, went to his gym bag, and took out some baby oil. He oiled his butt, straddled Dean's upright cock, and slowly eased himself down onto it. "Ah-h-h-h-h . . . Oh, man, that feels so fucking good. You have no idea how long I've wanted to do this!"

"You've been wanting—?" Dean freaked out; he couldn't believe what he was hearing! For a moment he thought maybe he was dreaming, but when Mike's ass tightly grasped his cockshaft and a tingle raced along his spine, Dean knew it was all for real. "Oh, fuck," he exclaimed, "you are something, Mike! You are really something!"

"Damn right I am," Mike roared. Slow and easy at first, then harder and faster, he started bouncing up and down on Dean's fat dick. His asshole was smooth as silk but tight, real tight, and in no time Dean was ready to unload.

"What a fucking piece of meat, Dean! So fucking big. You're going right up my asshole and filling me up! Yeah, stretching my ass and filling my guts with your big, fucking dick!"

"Ahhhh!" Dean tried but couldn't, just couldn't hold out any longer. Rolling up, he grabbed Mike about the hips, driving the older man's ass down hard onto the steaming cock that was fucking him. Spurt after spurt of thick, syrupy cum surged up Dean's fuckpole and spewed into the muscle-stud, filling him until it started running back out again.

Mike slowly eased himself off Dean's cock, which was still hard, stood up, and shook out his muscles. He bent down and gave

Dean a kiss. "That was a great fuck, kid, really great. I needed it bad. Now, just lie back, take things easy and let your daddy show you a thing or two."

Using more baby oil, Mike covered Dean's body with a light coating so that even in the gym's dim light his muscles seemed to come alive with size, power and strength as they rippled and flexed under his thin layer of skin. "A bodybuilder likes two things, kid. He likes to fuck and he likes muscle, especially his own. Now, if he can combine the two, he's really got it made. Muscles and sex, there ain't nothing finer. Are you beginning to see what I mean?"

In awe, Dean nodded. Gazing up at the glistening bodybuilder, he thought he had never seen in his life anyone so magnificent, so incredibly sexy. And with Mike's fiery-red poker rising from between his legs to complete the picture, Dean was absolutely sure he had found the ultimate man. "Fuck me, Mike," he intoned, deep and guttural, like a chant. "Fuck the living daylights out of me!"

Mike pushed Dean's legs back, placed the slick head of his cock at the waiting pink asshole and said, "You got it, kid. All of it, all the way!" With that he grabbed Dean about the waist, and pushed.

It was all Dean could do to keep from yelling, Mike was so big. Oh, man, he wanted this fuck. He wanted Mike in him real bad.

Another long push and more of Mike's cock disappeared up Dean's hot hole. Another push and—"Ahhh!"—Mike's cock slid in right to the hilt, slamming his dangling, cum-laden, hairy balls against Dean's asscheeks. In triumph, his engorged cock stretching Dean's ass to the limit, Mike threw his head back and swung his flexed arms up in a double biceps pose.

"Oh, GE-E-E-E-E-E-Z!" moaned Dean. He couldn't believe it; he was getting the humpy stud's dick and a private posing display as well. He reached up to try and touch the glistening, rounded cannonballs of Mike's pumped arms. "Muscle . . . muscle . . . muscle," he whispered.

"Yeah, muscle," replied Mike. "Big, hard muscle." He relaxed, brought his arms down, and started pounding Dean's hot ass. "Muscles . . . muscle . . . muscle."

"Fuck me, muscle-stud, fuck me!"

"Yeah," grunted Mike, "I'll fuck you, kid. This daddy'll fuck you good."

"That's it! Oh, Daddy, fuck me and flex those big, sexy muscles. Big, sexy muscles. Real man's muscles! Flex!"

Mike hunkered down, blew some air and snapped into his second pose, a mind-blowing front abdominal shot. Three distinct rows of award-winning abdominal muscles popped into view across his stomach. They looked like a relief map of the Rocky Mountains. Incredibly, without missing a stroke or once slipping out, his monster cock continued its rhythmic assault on Dean's eager ass. Whomp! Whomp! Whomp! It slid in and out as though doing a quick set of exercises, as if doing more and more reps would make it bigger than it already was. Whomp! Whomp! Whomp!

Dean thrashed around on the bench like a harpooned shark, beside himself with the all-engulfing pleasure and pain. He'd never been fucked like this before, never this good. Never by a man who was everything he wanted. Never!

Sweat streamed off Mike in torrents; the heat and humidity of the gym were having their effect. He relaxed his abdominal pose and wiped the moisture from his face. Not once did he take his eyes off Dean. Not once did he let up on his slow, steady, unrelenting pounding. His aching dick kept plunging again and again into Dean's tight hole, stretching it, filling it, all the while building the pressure in his own nuts until he thought his whole body would explode.

"Mike! Mike! Oh, God, I think I'm going to come again! Oh-h-h-h-h, fuck!"

Shaking his head, fighting back the on-rushing waves of pleasure/pain which wracked his body, Mike grunted, "So am I, kid!" He took a deep breath, set his fists under his rib cage and quickly hit a front chest pose, proudly thrusting his thick pectoral slabs up and out in front of him. "Fuck, I can't hold out much longer, kid!"

"Now! Shoot! Come in me!" cried Dean. "Ahhh!" The first wad of jism burst out of his raging cock and splashed across his heaving chest.

"Yes!" growled Mike. He started shaking as he fought to control himself. Almost in desperation, as if doing it would delay the inevitable, he abandoned the chest pose and hit a most-muscular. Suddenly he, too, cried out, tossed aside his posing routine and pounded Dean's ass like a rabid animal. "Yes! Yes! Yes! *Yes!*"

Dean let out a gasp. Mike's exploding jism was searing his insides. The hot cum felt like bolts of molten lead as Dean's guts were scrambled by the massive dick deep inside him. His asshole throbbed, feeling as though it was being worked over by a cattle prod. Too much, it was all too much!

When he came to, Dean was relieved to find that, no, he hadn't been dreaming. Mike was indeed with him, kneeling beside him, tenderly caressing the side of his face. "What happened? I feel like I was hit by a ton of bricks."

"How about 200 pounds of muscle?" smirked Mike. "Come on, you've had a rough night. Time to go home."

"Home?"

"Don't look so damned worried. You ain't going home alone, you're coming back to my place. No fucking way I'm going to let a future Mr. America out of my grasp. I ain't finished with you yet. Come on."

"Yes, Sir!"

No Pain, No Gain

BRAD MILLER IS THE biggest, strongest, most muscular bodybuilder in a gym full of big, strong, muscular bodybuilders. Barely into his thirties, he stands 5′10″, weighs 280 pounds and is built like a proverbial brick shithouse. Into the extreme bigger-is-better mindset, his stats border on the obscene: 57″ chest, 22″ neck, 23″ arms, 18″ forearms, 31″ waist, 32″ thighs, 24″ calves. He's a staggering example of a bodybuilder totally committed to doing whatever it takes to build mega-size, mega-mass and maximum definition. His workouts are brutal, gut-wrenching affairs where "no pain, no gain" is only the starting point. But the results speak for themselves. He's a monster. He is so big and freaky he even grosses out the gym's hardcores. Everyone, that is, except Pete.

To Pete, Brad Miller is masculine musculature personified. A fantasy come to life. Pete lusts after every big, freaky, mind-boggling inch of him. Trouble is, Brad won't even acknowledge his existence. There's a fair amount of eye contact (interesting how many times Pete catches Brad looking at him) but that's as far as it goes. Either Brad doesn't want to tarnish his tough, macho-straight reputation by associating with a suspected deviant or, more likely, he simply refuses to socialize with anyone who can't match his monstrous physical attributes (which would account for his aloof attitude to the world in general and Pete in particular). At 6′1″, 190 muscular pounds, the 38-year old Pete is in better shape than most but still, compared to Brad, he ain't nothing but a wimp. Too bad, Pete sighs wistfully, sometimes there's a lot more to a "wimp" than meets the eye.

It's a Friday night. Late, almost closing. As usual, only Pete, Brad and a few other die-hards are left. Brad's just about finished a grueling, two-hour chest workout. Name the exercise and he's done four sets of twelve reps with as much weight as he can handle. Makes the other guys look like a bunch of old ladies. He wears a shredded tank top that does nothing to cover his hairless sweat-drenched upper body. His brutally pumped, massive, monster pecs are hanging out in the open in all their bulging, ripped, vascular glory, driving Pete crazy with their formidable size and staggering mass. Out in the open, too, are his engorged thimble-sized nipples, their thick elongated development a riveting testimonial to long, involved workouts of an altogether different kind. Brad is obviously no tit novice.

He's got the vexing habit of massaging his enormous, overhanging pecs between sets to feel how big and pumped they're getting. And then, once satisfied they're truly fucking gigantic, he plays with his rigid throbnobs until he's ready to go at the weights again. He clearly enjoys twisting, tugging and pulling on his gorilla nips; at least, going by the contented smile on his otherwise tired face he does. It drives Pete up the frigging wall being so close and yet so far to those awesome pecs and mouth-watering nips. Maybe what frustrates Pete even more is the feeling that Brad is doing the tit-tugging deliberately, to tease him, knowing the effect it has on him. The bastard.

Finally Pete can stand it no longer and he flees to the relative safety of the deserted locker room. He needs a cold shower. A very long, very cold shower. He's down to his jockstrap when, to his stunned amazement, Brad lumbers in. Even more amazing, the behemoth casually strips down to a miniscule pair of briefs (which are pulled deep into the crack of his gigantic bubblebutt and barely contain his impressive party-sized equipment), takes a position in front of the mirror mere feet from where Pete is standing and starts hitting one mind-boggling pose after another. Double biceps. Front lat spread. Legs and abs. Boom. Boom. Boom.

Pete is blown away by this strange turn of events. What the fuck is going on? Their eyes meet a couple of times in the mirror but Brad keeps posing. Side chest. Side triceps. Relaxed full frontal. Boom. Boom. Boom. He's absolutely awesome, totally mind-blowing. Then, right in the middle of a double biceps, he holds Pete's gaze and asks pointblank, "So, do you think I'm big enough?" Without missing a beat Pete replies, "You're a fuckin' monster."

Brad nods with approval at the appraisal, then crabs into a most-muscular. "Yeah, I am," he agrees smugly.

"And those are the biggest, freakiest, hottest-looking nipples I've ever seen in my life. They're fuckin' perfect," Pete exclaims.

Brad stops posing and leans back against a row of lockers. Hands on hips, he looks down at each of his hard nips in turn, back up at Pete and growls, "Nothing's perfect. There's always room for improvement. That's where you come in. I know you want 'em. And tonight I'm in the mood to let you have 'em. Let's see what you can do. Work 'em and make me a happy man. And remember: no pain, no gain."

Pete grasps the massive curved pecs and gives them a firm all-over massage. This allows him the opportunity to not only admire their size and shape but gauge their thickness and density as well. He tells Brad to "Flex 'em!" and almost creams when the colossal mounds solidify into squared slabs of bulging rock-hard pec-muscle. He massages the slabs again in a kind of tactile "before" and "after" muscle comparison. He likes what Brad's got. His hard cock attests to that. Brad likes what he's doing, too, going by the bulge in his briefs.

Then Pete grips the thimble-sized nips and gently pulls and twists them back and forth. They're already pumped from the weight workout but under his expert manipulation he can feel the big rubbery nubs swell and grow even bigger and harder. Fuck, they are beauties. So beautiful he can't resist pinching them a little harder and rougher, adding just a touch more pressure with each measured twist of his hand. Then harder and rougher still, causing Brad's head to slump back and a soft "Ahhh" to escape from between the musclestud's lips. He pulls the turgid tit ornaments out from Brad's chest just to see how far they'll go, which ain't far considering how tight the skin is stretched across the heaving chest and then, curiosity satisfied, he pushes them down hard into the rippling pecmuscle, digging his thumbnails into the fleshy nubs for added stimulation. Beautiful.

Catching Brad completely off-guard, Pete suddenly delivers a series of sharp, stinging slaps with the flat of his hand to the defenseless pecnobs. Again and again, back and forth, harder and harder. He doesn't let up until the skin around the target area is glowing bright red and the tortured tits themselves are sizzling hot. Then, figuring the last thing Brad would expect after a serious tit-warming is a little tenderness, Pete slowly, gently, lovingly leans in and laps at the swollen, steaming nubs with his tongue. Sure enough, the muscular hulk lets out a whimper as first one and then the other delectable, inflamed nipple is carefully drawn into his warm, soothing mouth.

The succulent meaty morsels are like manna from heaven. The more of them Pete gets, the more of them Pete wants. In no time he starts losing it, totally losing it. The sucking becomes nibbling. The nibbling becomes nipping, which leads to light chewing which, try as he might to hold back, to linger, to enjoy the moment, develops into some major and very serious gnawing. He turns into a crazy man, a maniacal tit-loving pig. And just like when he uses his hands, Pete delights in varying his oral tit manipulation to get the biggest bang for his tit-loving buck. Between sucking, nibbling, nipping, chewing and gnawing, and by alternating between gentle and rough, hard and soft, fast and slow, he stokes the raging fire of his sexual furnace until he can barely contain either his sanity or the jizz in his balls.

Brad's getting off on the workout big-time, too. His briefs are down around his ankles and he's pounding his rock-hard, cum-dripping cock like there's no tomorrow. "Yeah, chew those tits. Harder. Harder!" he snarls. "Really chow down and let me feel some teeth. Yeah, that's it. That's it!"

Suddenly changing tack again, Pete steps back and wipes the spit off the bulging pecs, then latches onto the thick throbnobs with his fingers and proceeds to give them another expert going-over. Real controlled and efficient this time, even more thorough and unrelenting than before. A novice would call the workout extreme but Brad keeps moaning and beating his meat so Pete knows he's on the right track. He gets harder and rougher. His fingers are like vise-grips clamped onto the thick, elongated nipplenubs. They're brutal, continually twisting and pulling, stretching and tenderizing. Brad revels in the punishment and calls out for more. More and harder! More and rougher! More and—

Pete gives the sizzling pecnobs a really vicious twist and Brad contracts like he's been hit in the gut with a thousand volts of electricity. "OhFuckYes!" The monster groans as the pleasure/pain in his supercharged tits suddenly detonates the fiery jizzbomb in his ballsac and turns his throbbing cock into a cum-spurting volcano. "*OhhhFuuuuuck!*" Brad thrusts out his chest and flexes his pecs to maximize the intensity of his orgasm as his exploding cock drenches Pete with thick creamy jizz. "Twist 'em!" he gasps. "Twist my fuckin' tits right off! Yeahhh!"

Pete does as he's told. He keeps working the big rubbery pec-nobs until Brad milks every last bit of jizz from his red-hot cock and is reduced to a mountainous mass of quivering muscle. He lets go only when the monster slowly drops to his knees and falls back against the lockers, his massive chest heaving for air, his thick swollen nipples glowing a bright red.

Unable to withstand the craziness in his guts and the fire in his balls a moment longer, Pete hauls out his engorged cock and pumps the throbbing meat the same way he worked Brad's tits: hard and rough, with a passion that borders on the demonic. All he can see before him are the magnificent twin peaks of Brad's beefy big tits. Them and the massive, muscular pecs they sit on. He wants them, wants them bad.

Brad reaches up, seizes Pete's two pencil eraser-sized nips and—*boom!*—triggers the explosion in Pete's balls that detonates an orgasm of epic proportions and sends gobs of creamy jizz rocketing out his gaping pisshole. The gut-wrenching event is a mind-numbing one-two punch to the senses: searing white-hot pleasure/pain to his super-sensitive tits and rapid-fire rabbit punches to his contracting nuts. Exactly the way Pete likes his orgasms. In seconds, his balls are hanging low and empty and Brad's torso is spattered with glistening gobs of pearly-hued manseed. Lots of pearly-hued manseed. Drained, exhausted but filled with a wonderful feeling of peace and contentment, Pete drops to his knees and reverently spreads his slick, sticky cum all over Brad's chest and nipples—a special offering to the awe-inspiring pecs and inspirational tits of his deliverance.

Brad looks up from his chest and locks eyes with Pete. "Not bad," he says, "not fuckin' bad. You gonna be here tomorrow night?"

"I can be. Why?"

"Because I need a workout partner. Someone who can appreciate my need for a few extra, specialized routines. I think you've demonstrated a definite appreciation of that need."

A sly grin spreads across Pete's face. He reaches over and, giving the monster tits a playful tug, says quietly, "Believe me, Brad, when it comes to appreciation, you ain't felt nothin' yet!"

Texas Tits

WHEN HE FIRST STARTED on the loading dock, Tank really pissed me off. He knew it, too, even if he didn't know why. He worked extra hard to try and keep me happy, "Yes, Sir"-ing this and "No problem, Sir"-ing that, always wondering when I was going to snarl at him next. I laid the heavy-duty attitude trip on him partly because he was new and I wanted to make sure he figured out who was the boss, partly because I sensed he got off on taking orders, but mostly because he made me hornier than hell and I had to blow off steam somehow. I mean, my fuckin' cock ached just thinking about him.

His real name's Dominic, but after the first day on the dock the rest of the guys started calling him Tank. It's an apt description. He's one of the best-looking Texas boys I have ever laid my Texas eyes on, the kind that must have started lifting weights when he was three. He's only about 5′8″ but his 220 pounds—that's right, 220—is all solid fuckin' muscle. None of that sleek, candy-ass bodybuilder muscle, either. I'm talking enormous, over-sized, powerlifter-type muscle. The kind that gives a guy shoulders a yard wide, a bull neck, traps that start behind the ears, mountainous pecs you can set a beermug on, a massive back with lats so flared it's impossible for him to put his cannonball-sized arms down at his sides, a thick hard-as-rock gut, and thighs that would shame an elephant.

The kid is a fuckin' monster, some might even say grotesque, but he can do the work of two men and so quickly earned the respect of the others. Besides, beauty being in the eye of the beholder and all that shit, one man's grotesque is another's hunk of Grade-A Prime and, let me tell you, looking at Tank is like setting the thermostat in my balls on "High."

But like I said, the kid—and I call anyone who's only 25 a kid—really picked my ass. He was being a fuckin' cocktease. Here's this Texas boy guy loaded with muscle and for some mysterious reason he keeps most of it covered up. What the fuck gives?

It's ninety in the shade, everyone else is either in a T-shirt or stripped to the waist, and he's wearing a bulky flannel shirt! Sure, he's got the arms chopped off and most of the buttons undone, but he's still covering up the best fuckin' part of the male anatomy. Now, don't get me wrong, a hard cock and a tight ass are important but nothing beats two worked-over nipples on a set of bulging, muscular pecs.

The way he filled out his shirt I figured Tank's tits must have been nothing short of spectacular. So why the fuck wasn't he showing them off? It ain't natural for a guy with muscle to keep it hidden, especially around other muscular guys. This cutesy, coy crap had to stop and, as luck would have it, it was some of the other guys who gave me the chance to make my move.

A bunch of us were sitting around on the dock eating lunch and shooting the breeze when, as it always does on a Friday, the question came up as to who was going to the bar after work for a few beers. That always leads to a heated argument on the bar's strippers, which usually degenerates into a crude discussion on the finer points of a woman.

"I'm a cunt man," stated Vic Morowsky, for something like the tenth time. "Cunt is definitely the best part."

"No, man, you're wrong," argued Manny Montoya, shaking his head. "Ass. Ass is where it's at."

"You're full of shit," replied Morowsky. "Tank. Hey, Tank. What do you think is the best part?"

Tank is not a talker at the best of times, so being asked an opinion made him uncomfortable as hell. He looked around helplessly and shrugged those Herculean shoulders of his, unable to speak.

That's when I decided to play my hunch. Looking him in the eye, I said, "I'll bet Tank's a tit man."

The look of embarrassed surprise in Tank's brown eyes said it all. Guilty, as charged, Your Honor. His red face confirmed it.

I made a point of scratching my hard, quarter-inch left nipple through the fabric of my sweat-soaked T-shirt when I asked, "Am I right, Tank? Are you a tit man? Do tits turn you on?"

The rest of the guys roared in good-natured delight, getting a kick out of Tank's obvious unease, assuming he was shy but still one of them. I knew differently. The way he was staring at my tit and licking his lips told me the truth. I had him.

The horn signaling the end of lunch went off and the guys scattered to put their stuff away, giving Tank and me a few minutes alone. I walked up to him and he protectively crossed his arms over his broad chest.

"You didn't answer me, Tank," I growled. "Are - you - a - tit - man?"

Despite being bigger and stronger, Tank knew his place. He just didn't know me. After a long pause, his eyes downcast, he finally confessed, "Yes, Sir, I'm a tit man. I get off on tits, Sir."

"Especially your own?" I prodded.

His eyes met mine. They weren't shy any more. They were open and trusting, the eyes of a man confident that his secret was accepted and understood. "Take off your shirt," I ordered.

He did as he was told and boldly thrust out his tanned, hairless chest for inspection. Holy shit! The first time I laid eyes on his tits I just about crapped my drawers, I was so impressed. My wildest dreams had come true—ten times over. His massive pecs sat low and heavy across his deep ribcage, two sweeping slabs of densely packed muscle more majestic than any mountain range. And capping each rounded peak was a good half-inch of hard, mouth-watering nipple about as thick as the end of my baby finger.

I reached across and slid the palm of my hand over the curve of his left pec, feeling the warm satin-smoothness of his skin and the unyielding muscle beneath. First tracing a finger along the outer edge, I then grabbed a handful of the bulging muscle, all the while marvelling at its size, shape and density, and gave it a good, hard squeeze. In response, almost as if he was showing off, Tank contracted his pecs and the muscle solidified like concrete under my touch. Beautiful, simply fuckin' beautiful.

I knew I was running out of time so I reluctantly released the pec and let my fingertips drift over Tank's impressive left nipple, a prime example of prolonged workouts if I ever saw one. Rolling it between thumb and forefinger, I stated the obvious. "These are not virgin tits."

"No, Sir. They've seen a lot of action, Sir." Tank's voice dropped and he hesitantly asked, "Would Sir do me the honor of giving them a workout?"

When I didn't reply right away, and let go of his tit to boot (out of the corner of my eye I could see some of the guys coming back), Tank looked into my face and in a barely audible voice begged, "*Please*, Sir."

I let him stew a few more seconds, then said, "Meet me at my car after work."

"Yes, Sir."

"Oh, and keep your shirt off," I added. "I want to be able to see those tits this afternoon."

"But, Sir," he stammered, "the guys, uh, they'll see, too. They won't . . . understand."

"Fuck the guys," I sneered. "It's me you gotta worry about."

"Yes, Sir. I'm sorry, Sir."

So that afternoon Tank worked with his shirt off. And man, let me tell you, my fuckin' balls burned every time I caught sight of those sweat-drenched pecs and gorilla-sized nipples. Maybe even more of a turn-on was watching how the other guys reacted to seeing Tank's tits. There was everything from stunned surprise to horror and disgust. Everybody looked, some stared, but no one had the guts to say anything out loud.

And Tank? Yeh, he was self-conscious at first. But as the day wore on his confidence grew and by the end of the shift, even his bulky, over-sized jeans (he needs 'em for his thighs) couldn't hide the hard-on he was sporting.

As ordered, he was waiting by my car at the end of the day. Without a word, I used his shirt to wipe the sweat off his pecs, then reached into my lunch bucket for a couple of tiny, chrome-plated clothespins. I snapped them onto his tits, thinking they looked damn insignificant on the huge expanse of chest and knowing they were pretty Mickey Mouse for a guy with Tank's experience, but Tank let out a low moan and seemed to get off on them nonetheless, so I stopped worrying. I told him to get in.

Twenty minutes later, he was standing naked before me in my basement playroom waiting for whatever I had in mind. He looked fuckin' impressive. I ran an appraising hand over his shoulders, back, tight bubblebutt and tree-trunk thighs. This was going to be good.

I reached down and grabbed his cut, cum-dripping cock. It's just like him: short (maybe five inches) but thick, real thick. Imagine a sawed-off beer can and you'll know what I mean. I pumped it slow and rough-like a couple of times to get the feel of it, then slid down to grab his low-hanging bullnuts and give them a twist. Nice, real fuckin' nice.

I couldn't help smiling inwardly when I pulled the chrome clothespins off Tank's tits and his eyes blissfully glazed over for a moment as the blood rushed back into them. Talk about tit-sensitive! Fuck, if this is how the kid reacts to the Mickey Mouse stuff, I thought, he's going to freak when we start going heavy-duty. But I quickly reminded myself that going heavy-duty was a long, long way off yet and that even with a man of Tank's experience the pleasure of going from A to Z is hitting every letter in between.

With that in mind, and knowing how anybody who lifts weights gets off on his own pumped muscles, I led Tank over to the bench press and told him he was going to warm up by cranking off eight reps.

"Yes, Sir," he replied, sliding smugly under the 200-pound barbell.

"But before you start," I said, "these are to remind you to concentrate on your pecs." His eyes widened and his smug little grin vanished when he saw me pick up a couple of mean-looking, rubber-tipped alligator clamps from a nearby work bench and hold them a moment for his inspection.

He hoped gritting his teeth would help but, no, he still ended up wincing in pain when I eased first one, then the other clamp onto his tingling tits. "There, that'll help," I taunted. "Now, squeeze out them reps."

Like I knew it would be, the set was a piece of cake for him. Fine, let him think he was finished. I tapped the ends of his nipples (which made his cock jump and brought a nice whimper to his lips) and ordered him over to the incline bench, where I told him to use the thirty pound dumbbells and squeeze off eight reps of incline flyes, another great chest exercise.

Before Tank could open his mouth to complain, I gave the clamps a good twist to remind him who's boss. He let out a howl and I barked, "Is there a problem with that?" He obediently shook his head and, with his concentration focused back on his pecs, sat on the incline bench and did the flyes in strict form like a good boy.

He was a beautiful sight pumping that iron. His huge pecs alternately contracted and relaxed across his broad chest, his shoulders writhed in a blatant display of power and strength, and his cannonball arms grew to near-inhuman proportions. The man was a monster. But he was *my* monster.

And if I thought the muscle show was a beautiful sight, then watching those clamps turn Tank's swollen tits into concentrated pain receptors was nothing short of friggin' fantastic. They were tenderizing those tortured nipples real good and searing a memory of that workout into his brain he'd never forget. By the look on his face, I could tell he was hurtin' something fierce.

But if his face said one thing, his fat, vein-popping cock said another. It belied Tank's pained expression by pointing up at me like a loaded howitzer just itchin' to go off. All Tank needed was someone to pull the trigger. And, dammit, that someone was going to be me.

I had Tank repeat the exercises four times. He was exhausted by the time I finally let him stop but, man, you should have seen his chest, shoulders and arms. He was pumped bigger than a fuckin' house!

He looked so hot I was having real trouble controlling my baser instincts. I stripped down to a sweaty, piss-stained jockstrap and, let me tell you, the way my hard cock and aching balls were screaming for relief, it was all I could do to keep from throwing Tank down and fuckin' him right then and there. So I did the next best thing. I took the clamps off his tits.

Sure enough, Tank's pecs were so pumped and his tits just tender enough that when the blood hit the nerve endings in his nipples, it zapped him like a bolt of lightning. He let out a howl and just about doubled over.

"No you don't!" I yelled. "Stand up! I want them tits pointing skyward! And keep your fuckin' hands at your sides!"

I gotta hand it to the kid, he might have had tears in his eyes but he stood up and thrust out his chest like a man. And he stayed like that, too, when I started grabbing handfuls of those heavy slabs and massaging the piss out of them and pounding them with my fists and just generally giving his chest the how-do-you-do once-over.

Before long I could feel Tank responding, flexing those pecs and resisting my rough attention. That's right, kid, I thought, fight me.

Fight me hard. But Tank wasn't fighting and I knew it. Just the opposite. Any man with muscles welcomes the chance to show off the results of his work, to be inspected and compared, to be admired. I respect that.

"Okay, flex," I ordered. "Tighten those pecs. Come on, Tank, let me feel those pecs bust outta that skin. Impress me, man. That's right, fuckin' impress me!"

When he hunkered down into a most-muscular I grabbed those large inviting nipples of his and spun them back and forth like dials to help him along. "That's it, kid. Keep flexin'. Flex 'em hard! Harder! Now, hold it. Hold it right there!" While he held the contraction, I bent down and took his left nipple between my teeth for some immediate oral satisfaction. In no time I had him moaning and groaning and gasping for breath.

Sometimes I'd gently nip at those big ol' nubs real delicate-like with my front teeth and other times I'd suck them deep into my mouth and grind them, grind 'em good. And then sometimes, for a nice change of pace, I'd flick over them with the end of my tongue, tickling the red-hot nips just enough to let him know I was there (which, after all the rough stuff, seemed to drive Tank the craziest). It's true, you know, sometimes less is more.

The way my balls were churnin' I knew I wasn't going to last too much longer that time around. I took a quick glance at the glistening strands of pre-cum dripping from Tank's piledriver and figured he was damn close, too. Time to go out with a bang, I thought.

I chewed on his tits a few more seconds, then told him to go lie down on the bench while I pulled off my jock and picked up a few toys. Then, telling him to hold onto the bar above his chest with a wide grip, I fastened a couple of Dutch Demons to his tits and draped the four-foot connecting chain over the bar so that about a foot of it ended up hanging down on the other side. He let out a low, guttural moan when I clipped some weight on the chain and his tits were stretched up from his chest. The expression of pained pleasure on his face was downright heart-warming. Man, I could hardly wait until we really got going and that weight started jumping up and down and jerking like crazy on those clamps. The teeth would make mincemeat outta those tits and then he'd really be fuckin' ecstatic!

As for me, my dick damn near exploded when I attached an alligator clamp to one nipple, looped the thin connecting cord around my cock and balls and attached the second alligator to my other nipple. The cord was just the right length so that every time I stretched my torso there'd be a good yank on my tits. Ha, Tank wasn't the only one who was going to have some fun. I slipped on a condom, slapped on some lube and hefted Tank's stocky legs onto my shoulders, exposing his pretty pink asshole to the light of day.

Tank's pearly gate was a tight little fucker. I knew he was trying to be sociable and relax, but my dick's on the big side so it took some time and a lot of pressure before I could slip my cockhead past his sphincter into his shitchute. All the while, he's moaning and groaning and rolling his head back and forth and I can tell he's loving every intense minute of it.

Once my cockhead was in, though, I decided I'd been Mr. Nice Guy long enough and it was time to get down to some serious fuckin'. I took a deep breath and, with a grunt, rammed my cock right to the balls up that tight turdtunnel in one quick, gut-bustin' thrust.

Going by the look of wide-eyed surprise on his face, you'd've thought Tank had never been fucked before. He let out a holler, his knuckles went white gripping the bar and I thought my dick was a goner the way his ass clamped down on it. The man sucked me into his butt.

Even better was how my tits felt once I got going in my fucking Mode, what with the way the alligator clamps' teeth bit into them and tugged them every time I buried my dick in Tank's ass. My tits were on fire, they were hurting so good. And like they always do, the flames in my tits fanned my burning balls. It wouldn't be long now . . .

Tank looked like he was having the time of his life. He was right into getting his ass royally fucked now and I could tell that the clamps on his tits, with their added weight, were speeding him right along where I wanted him to be. He was fuckin' awesome the way his muscles contorted and writhed all over his tanned upper body, the way his over-sized tits were caught in the clamps and pulled up from his carved pecs, the way his skin glistened with sweat under the dim lights and that look of total tit-induced absorption on his face. Fuck, he was hot!

By now I was panting like a bellows and sweating like a pig as I shoved my cock again and again into Tank's tight bubblebutt. When my balls had a sudden spasm I gasped, "Any second now! Any fuckin' second!" and started pounding harder and faster.

"Fuck me, Sir! *Fuck me*!" Tank grunted as he unclipped the clamps from his tits. Just like before, only worse, when fresh blood hit those starved nerve endings he roared "*Ohfuck!*" and started thrashing around like he was getting hit with 20,000 volts.

He reached down, barely touched his cock and it was spurtin' thick, creamy wads of cum all across his abs and chest. Some even hit him in the face, there was so much force behind it. I was right, he did have a fuckin' howitzer between his legs!

All this thrashing and bucking around triggered a mind-blowing explosion in my own balls. Throwing back my head to give a good hard tug on my tits, I let out a roar to match Tank's and damn near passed out as I was hit with one heavy-duty contraction after another. A steaming load of jism rocketed up my cock and blasted out my pisshole deep into Tank's heaving gut. It's a good thing the latex was "Extra-Strength" because it felt like I was shooting bullets!

Man, it took a long time for Tank and me to recover from that first workout. Sometimes the first is the best. I'm happy to say that ain't so in our case. I know it sounds corny, but it just keeps getting better. We had a good time that weekend, getting to know each other in and out of the playroom. Turns out we were both what the other was looking for.

You should have seen Tank at work the following Monday. I made him wear his tightest T-shirt so that even when he was standing still there'd be some pressure on his super-sensitive tits and he'd keep remembering the weekend. And when he moved around, man, he was in absolute fuckin' agony.

Now, unless I tell him to, he won't wear a shirt at work. He's proud of his pecs and the big, worked-over nipples on them. On Fridays, when we're all sitting around having lunch and talking about strippers and which is the best part and all, Tank'll look me right in the eye and say "Tits." And Tank ought to know. He's got the tweakiest tits in the State of Texas.

What *I* have is Tank . . .

Strike Zone

THE BUSINESS END of a Spanish riding crop flicked with devastating precision against a nipple already chewed red and raw by vicious, jagged-toothed tit-clamps. A long, agonized howl filled the air. Stretched naked in a wide X between the upright wooden posts, Dave writhed in tormented convulsions at the cruel violation of his sensitive flesh, but there was little he could do to change the situation. The tight leather straps guaranteed that.

"You don't sound like such a cocky sonofabitch now," sneered the sweaty 6′4″, 280-pound monster Marine administering the discipline. He slowly, almost tenderly, trailed the rigid crop, the instrument of punishment, down Dave's heaving torso, along the sides of the weighted, swaying balls, and up the length of straining rock-hard cock, clearly satisfied with the pain and terror he was inflicting.

"And hell, I've only just begun," he smirked sadistically. A quick twist of the wrist and the crop bit deep into the defenseless, throbbing cockhead.

"Oh fuck, the pain!" Dave cried out again as he strained against his bonds in a futile attempt to channel the suffering from his body. No such luck. He had always thought himself one tough customer, able to withstand just about anything a talented S might dish out, but with Trask it was like he was back in M boot camp, like he'd never experienced a little discomfort before.

It was all his own fault, he acknowledged between labored gasps. Right from their first meeting he knew Trask was a master at measuring a man, testing his resolve, probing his mental and physical capabilities before neutralizing him at his weakest point, and leaving him defenseless and malleable. He knew that a man like Trask allows a "cocky sonofabitch" more than enough rope to hang himself before giving the rope a good yank to put him in his place. He knew all that, knew it and understood it, but he still thought he could outfox the hulking Marine wrestling coach. Maybe even turn the tables on him. Yeah, sure.

Dave thought of the old adage: pride goeth before a fall. When Trask walked into the locker room and caught him fucking that private's pretty little ass he should have acted sorry and contrite and maybe the whole thing would have blown over with a light slap on the wrist. After all, he could hardly get into trouble over a little recreational butt-fucking with someone who presides over regular Loser Gets Fucked practice matches. But no, pumped on raging hormones and hungering for a piece of the monster, he had decided to cut through the bullshit and throw caution to the wind.

Trask fumed in silence until the private hightailed it and then growled, "The men on this team are under your care and guidance so they can become champion wrestlers, Harrison. Not to provide you with an outlet for getting your rocks off."

Dave looked the Marine right in the eye and replied, "Excuse me, Sir, but it was Madison who needed the outlet. He was tense, Sir. *Very* tense. He needed to release his tension or he was going to explode. Just as, if I may be so bold as to point out, you need to release yours, Sir."

Trask's eyes narrowed to cold, reptilian slits. "My what? Tension?"

"Yes, Sir."

"Before I explode?"

"Yes, Sir."

"And I suppose, as team trainer, you're just the man to do it? Release my tension, that is."

Dave brazenly appraised the hulking musclestud. The view was intoxicating: a skin-tight, olive green T-shirt molded to massive, overhanging pecs; thimble-sized nipples; broad, barndoor shoulders tapering to a wasp-waist; huge, cannonball arms; colossal thighs; carved calves; scuffed size-13 hightops; and skimpy, red USMC shorts barely containing a thick cut cock, bull balls and a mouth-watering bubblebutt of classic proportions. It was the kind of view that makes a shambles of any kind of clear-headed thinking. Leering suggestively, Dave went for the gusto and threw down the gauntlet. "Isn't that why you had me transferred to this stinking hellhole, Captain? You've got a bad itch and you heard I'm the best man in the Corps when it comes to scratching."

"You are definitely too fucking much, mister. Too damn fucking cocky for your own good. But rest assured, when I get through with you, you won't be able to pick your own nose let alone scratch my itch. You'll know the meaning of the word respect."

"Respect, Sir, is both given and earned."

Trask ignored the comment and walked over to a padlocked door at the end of the locker room. He opened it, turned on a light and stepped to one side. "Get in."

Dave had always wondered what was behind the door. Suddenly he wasn't so sure he wanted to find out. "Why?" he mumbled. "What's in there?"

"I—said—get—in."

Swallowing hard, Dave did as he was told. "Ohhh, fuuuck."

It wasn't the largest or best-equipped playroom he'd ever seen but it definitely had everything needed to show a guy a good time. He took a deep breath to steady his nerves, not knowing which was worse, the fear in his gut or the fire in his balls. In seconds Trask had his wrists and ankles bound by thick leather straps to the two upright posts in the center of the room so that, really, it didn't matter either way.

In even less time, Dave's balls (which are low-hangers to begin with) were swaying lower still, courtesy of a leather pouch filled with ball bearings looped around his nutsac. Then his taut, dime-sized nipples were being savaged by not one but two pairs of sharp-toothed electrical clips.

Trask took a cat-o'-nine tails down from its place on the wall and said, "What say we loosen you up some? One hundred ought to do it."

"If you think that'll be enough, Sir," replied Dave, trying to ignore the mounting discomfort.

Trask's expression remained a blank. "I think it'll be a start."

It was more than a start, a lot more. It was a tribute to the power of the lash, a celebration of the power and finesse of an experienced whip handler. By the fiftieth stroke, what with the varied combination of rhythms, target areas and applied strengths, Dave knew he was in the hands of a master. By the seventieth, he was whimpering like a baby.

Although Trask concentrated on Dave's upper back and shoulders he wasn't averse to laying a few strokes on Dave's outstretched arms, clenched asscheeks or tensed thighs for variety's sake. And

Dave found it wasn't always the hard strokes that hurt the worst, either. A stroke lighter than expected, one out of sequence, or not there at all could be more torturous than a hard stroke delivered on cue to the most sensitive part of his body. By the time Trask reached one hundred, Dave was hanging limp as a rag from the posts, a heaving, reddened mass of smarting nerve endings.

Flushed from his exertion, Trask stripped off his sweat-drenched T-shirt and shorts and used them to mop his brow while he caught his breath, and contemplated his handiwork. Despite his obvious physical conditioning, the heat and humidity in the playroom's close confines were getting to him.

With one big paw-like hand tugging away on the half-gorged hunk of meat draped over his bull balls, Trask used his free hand to caress Dave's tingling backside. He seemed to approve of the way Dave winced when he grabbed a handful of warm ass cheek and gave it a good, hard squeeze. "What's the matter, Harrison?" he growled. "Your ass a little tender right about now?"

"Yes, Sir," grimaced Dave. He was almost in tears, Trask was digging into his butt so hard. "But that's okay, Sir, I like it . . . a little tender."

"Is that a fact?"

"Yes, Sir!"

"Well, maybe I should tenderize it a little more then," sneered the monster.

Dave let out a silent scream as he was pushed over another pain threshold. He met Trask's flashing eyes and, struggling for self-control, gasped, "That would be . . . nice, Sir."

"Good. Because I've got just the thing for this ass."

The Thing turned out to be a cricket bat, an elongated paddle-like piece of sports equipment designed for hitting a ball but, as they both knew, equally suited to warming a bare butt. Dave's stomach rose in his throat when Trask held the bat up for his inspection.

"Beautiful, isn't it?" Trask lovingly ran the palm of his hand down the bat's long, leather covered flat surface. "I got it—in more ways than one—from a Royal Marine when I was a kid stationed in England. He was a mean fucking sonofabitch. First time he used it on me I couldn't sit down for two days. My ass damn near glowed in the dark, it was so hot. It's the perfect training tool. And I can't think of anyone who needs it more than you, Harrison."

"If . . . you think it'll help, Sir."

"I do. Believe me, I do."

Whap! The bat landed flush on Dave's rounded butt cheeks with devastating accuracy, flattening them like pancakes and shocking each and every nerve ending.

Dave screamed, stunned by the heart-stopping power of the blow. He was propelled forward like a shot, back arched, every muscle contracted in bold relief, only to be stopped short by the cruel inflexibility of his restraints, and left to writhe like a stuck pig.

Pain, oh fuck, there was lots of pain! It was incredible, like nothing Dave had ever experienced before. All from one little paddle! His ass blazed with the heat of a raging fire, tingled from the thrusts of a thousand invisible knives and threatened to overwhelm his already beleaguered senses. To add to his misery, his weighted balls had been painfully jerked back and forth between his legs in a prime example of physics in motion, further straining his sac, torturing his nuts and inflaming his dick. If the paddling continued with the same intensity, his swaying gonads would be dragging on the floor in no time.

"Effective, isn't it?" Trask whispered.

"Yes, Sir," gasped Dave.

"I thought you'd like it." Whap!

"Ahhh!"

Whap!

"Ahhhhhh!"

Whap!

"Ahhhhhhhhhhhhhh!"

When Dave regained consciousness he discovered to his dismay that, while the paddling had stopped, he was still bound hand and foot to the posts and the searing pain radiating from his ass and short-circuiting his brain was no dream. It was real. Very, very real. Just as the pains in his arms and shoulders, his throbbing balls, aching dick, rubbery legs and parched throat were real. Fuck, there wasn't a single part of his body that didn't hurt!

Trask, in all his naked, sweating, monster-muscular glory was leaning against the wall directly in front of him, gently stroking his ten fat inches and sucking back a cold can of beer. "About time you came around. Thirsty? You are? You want a drink? Open your mouth."

Dave wasn't expecting Trask to take a big slug of beer and just spit it into his gaping mouth. Most of the golden liquid was long gone by the time he shut his trap. His humiliating loss and his raging thirst brought him close to tears. But then, in a surprising move that did bring tears to his eyes, Trask took another big slug, gently pressed his lips against Dave's and carefully passed the beer at a rate Dave could handle.

Dave slaked one thirst, then with his tongue tried to slake another. Trask pulled back and said softly, "Remember, I've got everything you need and want. Everything."

"Yes, Sir."

Trask paused a moment to let his words sink in before yanking the clamps off Dave's tits and allowing himself a moment to enjoy the agony of fresh blood oozing from the raw, tortured nipples. Taking a riding crop down from its wall hook, he drew the end of it along Dave's jaw and whispered, "All we have to do now is work out the terms."

If Dave had a healthy respect for the coarse, mind-numbing properties of a paddle, he harbored a particular dread for the precise, rapier-sharp talents of a riding crop. Try as he might, its ability to concentrate excruciating pain with pin-point accuracy on his body's smallest, most sensitive areas was something Dave had never gotten used to, much less mastered or controlled. And because the pain was so specific and so blindingly intense, his fear of the pain was almost as bad as the pain itself. The first stroke reconfirmed the worst.

"Aieeeee!"

The second and third strokes pushed Dave to the edge of a frightening new world. With only a few well-placed strokes to his ass, back, chest, arms and inner thighs, Trask reduced Dave to a whimpering, blubbering manchild who, between sobs and gasps, begged and pleaded with the monster to stop. The reply to the pleading was a quick flick of the crop to Dave's right tit, which elicited another long, agonized howl of pain.

"You don't sound like such a cocky sonofabitch now," Trask sneered, drawing the crop down Dave's heaving torso. "And hell,

I've only just begun," he smirked sadistically. Then he whacked Dave's cockhead. Right on the tip of the engorged, plum-sized head. Right smack across the gaping, cum-dripping pisshole. Dave snapped against the restraints as if he'd been zapped by 50,000 volts and let out a scream to wake the dead. The mind-blowing fireworks going off in his brain were almost as brutal as the excruciating pain radiating from the tip of his tenderized cock. Between the two points, he thought he was going to die. In fact, he almost wished for death.

Twap! The leather tip bit deep into the taut, elongated nutsac, midway between the base of the shaft and the bunched balls, causing yet another sudden jerk. Dave's convulsed body went one way, his balls another. "Aiieeee! Omigod, Sir! Stop, Ahhh, please stop! Pl—pl—pl—plea—"

No such luck. Twap! Twap! Twap! Both asscheeks and (in a skillful piece of crop handling) his frenum got it next. "Aiiieeeeeeeee!"

Three more shots—two to the back of his thighs, one to the crack of his ass—and Dave practically went out of his mind. Beside himself with pain, he was barely able to get a half-decent breath, what with all his choked sobs and fretting over where the next blow would land.

An even scarier thought pushed its way into Dave's fevered brain. He was positive that whatever self-control he had left was rapidly slipping through his cerebral fingers. At any moment he was going to snap, step over the edge and lose it completely. Perhaps forever. Just snap and . . .

"Please, Sir! Don't! Please, stop! Plea— Ahhhhh!"

But the expected blow never came and Dave was left hanging limp in his restraints, sobbing his guts out.

"There, there," cooed Trask. "It's going to be all right. Hey, don't worry, Harrison. I said everything's going to be all right."

Dave sniffed and choked back the sobs, valiantly trying to compose himself. Through watery eyes he peered at the man who had reduced him to this sorry state. He should hate the monster for what he had done, for having put him through this torture, this hell. But he couldn't.

Gazing at the strong, ultra-masculine face, drowning as he was in the swirling pools of the man's hypnotic black eyes, hate was the last emotion Dave felt.

Big, callused hands slid down to the weight-filled sack dangling from his nuts, unhooked it and tossed it aside. First Dave let out a sigh of relief for no longer having what felt like two tons tied around his balls (not that it felt like they snapped right back into place once they were free, either). Then he let out a low groan of pleasure-pain when a hand cupped his throbbing low-hangers and started rolling them around like dice in a crap game. To even Dave's amazement, fresh blood rushed to his dick and in no time it was standing ramrod straight again. "You just never fuckin' get enough, do you, Harrison?"

"Ummm . . . No, Sir. I guess not, Sir. Sorry, Sir."

Trask walked around back and snorted, "Well, maybe you'll get this."

For an experienced ass like Dave's, Trask's finger (large as it was) was nothing. Two fingers only got Dave more excited and he started pushing back on the digits harder and harder. Two fingers and a thumb—now that Dave felt. He let out a groan and rolled his head from side to side to counteract the mounting pressure. The invigorating, wonderful pressure.

But then, unexpectedly, the fingers were gone and Dave's gaping hole was empty, barren, yearning to be filled. Dave pushed back with his ass, as if his yawning sphincter might, somehow, magically suck in something big and hard to fill it, satisfy it, all the while letting out a series of pathetic little whines and whimpers.

The big, callused hands suddenly grabbed Dave's hips and roughly pulled his asscheeks apart. "Is this what you want?"

"Aiieeeeee!" A train, a big fucking train was going up Dave's ass! A big fucking monster freight train!

"What's the matter, Harrison?" grunted Trask, slowly pulling out a bit before—wham!—shoving his ten fat inches right back up Dave's shitchute. "I thought this is what you wanted, Corporal. Isn't this what you wanted? Didn't you want me pounding my big Marine pud up your pretty little ass? Didn't you?"

"Yes . . . ugh! . . . Sir!"

"What?"

"Yes . . . ahhh! . . . Sir!"

"*What?*"

"Yes, Sir! *Ahhhhhh!*" An invisible hand took hold of Dave's nuts and gave them a sudden, excruciating twist. A bomb went off in the bloated, churning sac and Dave lost it, totally fucking lost it. His whole body convulsed as thick, creamy wads of burning jism spurted in rapid-fire succession from his aching, rock-hard cock and his ass clamped down on his shitchute's violator, as much to hold it in place as to try and force it out.

Between the hot ass chewing on his dick and his bull balls crying out for relief, it was only a matter of seconds before Trask hit his own flashpoint and erupted. With his fuckpole jammed in all the way and his arms wrapped around Dave in a crushing bearhug to keep it there, Trask held on tight while his monster meat blew a load of molten manseed deep into Dave's churning guts.

"Uh! Oh fuck, yeah! Yeah! Fuck, yes! *Ahhhhhhh!*"

Spent, Trask ground his hips a couple of times to squeeze the remaining cum from his softening horsedick before yanking out and staggering back. Drenched in sweat, muscles pumped to the max, he stumbled around to face Dave and slumped against the nearest wall.

"Not bad, Corporal," he gasped, gulping down one deep breath after another. "You ain't the best fuck I've ever had but I can see why you're popular with the men."

Stung by the deliberate cruelty of the remark, Dave hung his head and murmured, "I'm sorry, Sir. I'll try harder next time."

Trask gave a grunt. "If there is a next time."

Dave looked up fearfully. "Please, Sir, I really will try harder. I . . . I want to please you. I want to make you happy. I do. You're right, you really are everything I want and need. Please, give me another chance."

Without answering, Trask came over and unfastened the straps binding Dave's ankles and wrists. Too weak to stand on his own, Dave crumpled in a heap on the wooden floor with the side of his face coming to rest mere inches from the splayed toes of Trask's big right foot.

The pungent aroma of sweaty, smelly, dirty feet galvanized Dave's already overloaded senses and activated still deeper, baser, barely-acknowledged instincts. Moaning, he stretched forward and took deep, heavy whiffs of the manstink until, salivating like a crazed dog and unable to hold back any longer, he used his quivering lips and broad, flat tongue to lovingly wash and lick Trask's size 13s.

"That's it, Harrison. Lick 'em. Lick 'em clean. Get right in there, right between every toe. Wash 'em, wash 'em good. Atta boy. Lick up every drop of sweat, every particle of dirt, every piece of toe-jam. I want them looking like I just stepped outta the tub.

"Good. Good boy. Now get up. Up on your knees, Harrison, and clean my cock. It's fucking filthy after poking your shitty little hole."

Dave knew his ass was squeaky clean when Trask fucked him but he wasn't about to argue the point. Besides, the chance of getting Trask's hefty hunk of dangling moose meat in his mouth was not to be delayed. Fuck, even soft it was bigger than most hard dicks.

"Yeh, that's right, Corporal. Suck it. Suck that meat. Clean it off real good. Suck all that shit and crap off it. Lick it. Lick— Hey, watch the teeth! I know it's big but *no teeth!*"

"Sorry, Sir. I'm sorry."

"Shut up. Now my pits. Stick your nose right in there and lick 'em clean. Yeh, that's right, suck up all that sweat. Man sweat, yeh. The sweat I worked up working you over. You caused it, you lick it up."

Dave happily kept licking away at the hairy armpits until he felt a shudder run through the monster. Pulling away, he looked into Trask's face and saw turmoil in the dark, piercing eyes.

Dropping his arms, Trask murmured, "That's enough. Enough but not enough. It's just . . ." Trask looked strangely uncomfortable. "I mean, needs and wants can cut both ways."

"I know." Dave waited. He had no intention of making it easy for the man.

"I . . . I do have an itch."

"Yes?"

"And you're right. I did get you here to scratch it. You have to scratch it."

"I don't have to do anything. But ask me and I might."

"Ask you? I don't think . . ."

"Say it."

Trask swallowed hard. This was shit or get off the pot time and he knew it. "I'm ready now. Help me, please?"

Idly running a hand over the massive, overhanging pecs with their big rubbery nipples, Dave let his eyes wander over the various pieces of equipment displayed on the walls until, having made up his mind, he pushed the monster back towards the two upright poles and said, "We'd better get started. It's going to be a long, long night."

Tarzan the Tit Man

MICK D'AMATO, the new kid in shipping/receiving, was a short, stocky little sonofabitch who one day got tagged with the nickname Tarzan. He got it not because he was Lord of the Loading Dock (even if, pound for pound, he was the strongest guy on it) but because he reminded some smartass lead hand of a small ape.

The kid got off on pumping iron and obviously spent a lot of time at the gym. He still had a lot to learn about balance and symmetry, however, because his broad shoulders, thick back, massive chest and cannonball arms were all over-developed and way out of proportion to the rest of his body, giving him a brutish, top-heavy physique. The imposing upper body musculature, coupled with the fact that he had a low hairline, deep-set eyes, pug nose, short bow legs and was covered by a dense mat of swirling black body hair only reinforced the simian resemblance. To Mick's chagrin, the moniker stuck. He didn't like it but there was dick-all he could do about it.

Pete Chernowski was the company's number one hotshot in Sales and Marketing. His office was up on the third floor, but he was often on the loading dock personally checking on his clients' outgoing orders. He damn near had a heart attack the first time he saw Mick.

The hirsute hunk looked primal, a real animal in more ways than one, and appealed to Pete at a basic, gut-wrenching level. Especially dressed as he was in a threadbare dirty white T-shirt that hugged his humpy muscular torso like a second skin and hid absolutely nothing from view. His monstrous curved pecs with their dark half-dollar size areola and huge cone-shaped nipples were, for all intents and purposes, right out in the open. It was all Pete could do not to jump the stud right then and there. He would have, too, except Mick unexpectedly turned and not only caught him staring *but stared right back!* It was too much. Pete beat a hasty retreat back to his office and whacked off to get his blood pressure back to normal.

Things got more intense each time Pete went down to the loading dock. First came the eye contact. It started out as feigned indifference but soon gave way to obvious interest (as obvious as two guys can get in a homophobic work environment). Then one morning Pete needed help getting a rush order together and a lead hand obligingly ordered Mick to assist. In an isolated corner of the warehouse Pete finally got his hands on Mick's impressive, mind-boggling chest. All it took was the admiring comment, "Big pecs." Mick pulled his T-shirt over his head, stuck his thumbs in his beltloops and replied, "Go ahead. Feel them."

Unmistakable proof of a hardcore weight room warrior, the awe-inspiring massively developed pecs were a chest aficionado's fantasy come true. They were unbelievably thick, incredibly dense and wondrously defined. There wasn't an ounce of fat on them. Even relaxed they barely moved. And, when Mick smugly flexed them for Pete's benefit and they solidified into two squared slabs of rock-hard, hair-covered manflesh, they didn't move at all. "Oh-h-h-h-fuck," said Pete.

Pete was practically hyperventilating, he was getting off on Mick's pecs so much. Then he burrowed through Mick's chest hair, found the hard rubbery nipples and gave them a gentle twist. Mick closed his eyes and practically purred. The purr deepened into a satisfied growl when Pete started twisting them like he really meant it. "Yea-a-h-h-h!"

Suddenly a lead hand called out, "Hey, Tarzan, where the fuck are you?" and the two men instinctively jumped apart. "Damn," Mick groused, yanking on his T-shirt. He gave Pete a wink, a whispered "See ya later" and called back, "What the fuck d'ya want?"

They couldn't talk for the rest of that day but Mick still found ways of keeping Pete's interest at a fever pitch. He started out by flexing his pecs whenever Pete came down to the dock. If the other guys were around he'd be subtle and tense them very discreetly, but if they were relatively secluded he'd give Pete a rousing, full-blown pec posing routine. He had the goods and, to Pete's delight, he knew how to show them off.

Sometime after lunch he fixed it so that his left nipple poked out of a large hole that had mysteriously appeared in his T-shirt. He might as well have poured gasoline on a smoldering fire showing off like that, he got Pete so horny.

Then, late in the afternoon, came the capper. Mick paused in the middle of dismantling an old shipping crate and, careful not to be seen by anyone else, took the pliers he was holding and used it to grab his exposed nipple, squeeze it, twist it back and forth and then stretch it out from his pec as far as he could, all the while making it very clear how much he was getting off on what he was doing. Pete got so turned on he could barely contain himself. Beside himself with frustration, he covered his raging hard-on with his clipboard, mouthed a silent "you bastard" and hustled off to plot his revenge.

Pete got his chance that very evening. He had stayed late to finish some paperwork. On his way out through the deserted warehouse, he found Mick, still busting his ass over a pile of old wooden pallets. In his scuffed workboots, skintight 501's and sweat-drenched, body-hugging dirty white T-shirt the stocky little powerhouse was an ultra-masculine wet dream. Even his pungent, funky mansmell was a turn-on.

"Hey, Tarzan," Pete taunted, "is that a banana in your pocket or are you just glad to see me?"

With a bemused smirk, Mick dropped what he was doing and turned to face his tormentor. Uttering a low, carnal moan, he peeled off his T-shirt, flexed his chest a couple of times and then without once breaking eye contact started massaging his big, overhanging pecs and playing with his thick, protruding nipples.

The invitation worked. Pete advanced until he had Mick backed up against a wall and then, carefully setting his attaché case down, he grabbed Mick about the waist, bent over and chewed on first one rigid oversized tit and then the other. It was a real labor of love for Pete and in no time he had Mick gasping for breath and writhing in frenzied rapture.

In the midst of his squirming Mick popped the buttons on his 501's and hauled out his cock and balls. Quite a hefty set of sex equipment was swinging in the breeze! He barely got his hand around his erect uncut hunk of manmeat when Pete swatted the hand away and growled, "No you don't. We got a long way to go yet before you blow."

A few minutes later, when the dockhand disobeyed him a second time, Pete took off his necktie and used it to bind Mick's hands behind his back. "There, that oughta hold you." Then he yanked Mick's pants all the way down to his ankles for good measure. The kid wasn't going anywhere now.

Pete was no beginner when it came to the advanced care and treatment of nipples and pecs. He brought his many talents and considerable expertise to bear in a tit workout experience that bordered on the religious. He started out massaging the huge, squared slabs of Mick's curved pecs, making sure they got the attention and respect they so richly deserved. He knew that any bodybuilder into his pecs gets off on having those pecs admired and appreciated and he was gratified to discover that Mick, perhaps even more than most, was definitely into muscle worship.

He had a fantastic time exploring the many extraordinary features of Mick's pecs. He pressed them, squeezed them and marvelled at the inhuman hardness and Herculean strength rippling beneath his fingertips. He revelled in their size and density when Mick eagerly tensed them for his benefit.

"Yeh, flex 'em. Flex those pecs for me," he snarled. "Let me feel you pump those pecs right in my hands!" Mick did as he was told.

Pete couldn't restrain himself any longer and he launched a serious assault on Mick's thick, cone-shaped nipples. Using only thumb and forefinger he played those big luscious nips for all they were worth. Most times he only twisted them back and forth. But by varying the intensity of his grip, by occasionally changing the rhythm and by once in a while doing something different, like pulling on the rubbery nubs as if he were milking a cow or digging his thumbnails into the meaty flesh until they almost disappeared into the quivering muscle, he kept Mick totally off-balance.The boy's tits were positively singing.

Mick was going ballistic. He moaned and groaned, rolled his head from side to side, gasped for breath and begged for more. He was insatiable. The more he got, the more he wanted. The more he wanted, the more he endured. His tits felt more alive than they'd ever been while, down at his crotch, his engorged, bloated cock throbbed something fierce and ached—no, screamed—for release. The fat bulbous knob was flushed an angry red and long gooey gobs of pearly-hued pre-cum oozed from the tip like sap from a maple tree. But with his hands bound behind his back,

Mick couldn't do a damn thing about it. No way could he get his rocks off tied up like that! His obvious frustration made Pete relish his work all the more and encouraged him to get a little rougher and tougher. He gritted his teeth, gave Mick a little smile and went through the routine again, increasing the intensity ten-fold. Mick's head fell back and a deep, guttural, "Yes-s-s-s!" rumbled up from his belly.

Just when Mick appeared unable to take any more, Pete removed his hands from the man's throb-knobs and took a step back to enjoy his handiwork and let the overheated hunk cool down a bit. Mick was a basket case. He was covered in sweat, his massive chest was heaving like a bellows and he was grunting like a frenzied ape. Maybe he had the right nickname after all. He was, indeed, a fucking animal. Deciding it was time to go for the gusto, Pete opened his attaché case and took out a pair of ordinary wooden clothespins.

Mick's face lit up like a roman candle. Pete liked the kid's craving for some serious titwork but decided a big man needed a big man's toys. He tossed the pins back and brought out a nasty-looking pair of chrome tit clamps joined by a foot and a half of thin chrome chain. The musclestud's anxious, wide-eyed expression of burning lust and desire as he stared at the instruments of pleasure/pain told Pete he'd struck paydirt. "Let's try these on for size," the bossman whispered.

Pete stretched out each engorged tit and carefully placed one of the wide-mouthed, small-toothed clamps as far down on the nub as it would go, leaving the top of the bloated, set-upon tit exposed to whatever else he had in store for it. Although the teeth were blunted by a protective latex cover, he knew from personal experience that the clamps bit into tenderized flesh with an especially cruel zeal. Even a hardened tit veteran could not take the punishment for long. The agonized expression on Mick's contorted, pain-wracked face told Pete the hunky musclestud would be no different.

"Here, hold this," Pete said as he placed the connecting chain, like a horse's bit, in Mick's mouth. Almost immediately Mick's head fell back and he started tugging on his tortured tits like a man possessed. Each concerted yank on the chain brought a louder and more agonized grunt as Mick himself increased the tempo and, therefore, the severity of the workout. Despite the pain radiating from his tormented tits Mick looked happier than a pig in shit. He was a man completely attuned to his needs and desires, a man happily achieving all those needs and desires.

But finally even Mick could take the unrelenting pleasure/pain no longer. He dropped the chain and cried out, "Oh God, Pete, let me come! Please, let me come! Grab my cock and get me off! Grab it, grab it just once and I'll shoot! That's all it'll take, I promise!"

"I'm sure it is," Pete said softly, "but I'm not quite finished yet." He reached into his attaché and brought out a regular soft-bristled toothbrush. "You'll be surprised how effective this is going to be right about now," he said.

Effective wasn't the word. Pete might as well have used the world's coarsest sandpaper, the way the nylon bristles played across the reddened tips of Mick's tenderized tits. The toothbrush definitely did the trick. Something inside Mick snapped and he went totally fucking ape-shit. He threw back his head, thrust out his chest and let go with an enraptured jungle roar of pure bestial pleasure. In that split second before he completely lost it Pete dropped the brush, took off the clamps and quickly suckled first one and then the other inflamed nipple in his warm, soothing mouth. Boom! The fresh blood flooding the hunky musclestud's engorged nipples triggered an incredible convulsion of epic proportions. His whole body was jolted by a series of staggering, muscle-wrenching contractions that must have measured close to 9.9 on the open-ended Richter scale. His cock, without so much as a finger on it, suddenly exploded in a brutal, ball-busting orgasm that sent wads of rich creamy cum rocketing like tracer bullets across the room.

Holy-fuckin'-jeezus! Each powerful contraction pummelled Mick as effectively as a real punch to the gut. He gave a loud animal grunt as the invisible fist hit him again and again and again. Each "blow" caused him to snap forward at the waist and involuntarily tense every big, bulging muscle in his body against the assault which, in turn, jerked his churning nutsac back and forth something fierce and sent yet another thick dollop of steaming jizz blasting out of his gaping pisshole. It was an awesome display of masculine below-the-belt firepower. Impressive to watch, the orgasmic overload must have been hell to endure. But Mick not only endured it, he welcomed it body and soul. He embraced it like the total man-beast he was.

"Ah! Ahh! Ahhh! Ahhhhhhh!"

"Aw fuck, Mick! That's it, that's fuckin' it! Shoot that load! Yes, shoot that big fuckin' load! Shoot it right into the next fuckin' state!"

Somehow in all his wild thrashing around, Mick managed to work his wrists free of his necktie bonds, get his clenched fists up to his chest and start pounding on his pumped pecs and hyper-sensitive nips. It was a wonder he didn't hurt himself, beating as hard as he did. But it must have been worth it, going by the look of sheer physical bliss on his drawn, ecstatic face, because he kept at it until his cock had blown its entire load and his empty nuts were practically dragging on the floor.

"Ahhhhhhhhhhhhhhhhhhhhhh!"

Spent but still adrenaline-charged, Mick let out a growl, grabbed Pete about the waist and hauled him in tight against his heaving, sweat-drenched muscular body for a prolonged, heavy-duty bout of "mano-a-mano" lip-lock. By the time he finally let Pete up for air they were both panting.

"You're a wild animal!" gasped Pete. "A crazy man."

"Yeah, you got that right," Mick smirked. "Play with my nipples and I go fuckin' ape."

"Tarzan the Tit Man," grinned Pete. He ground his hips into Mick's groin and in a deep, suggestive voice asked, "So, Tarzan, you wanna come back to my place and see what else I got in the case?"

Mick grinned back and replied, "Pinch my tits and I'll follow you . . . Ohhh-fuck-that-feels-good!"

"Hmmmm, I'll take that as a yes."

"Grrrrr-r-r-r-r-r!"

Hard Times

THANKS TO A LOUSY economy, the company I busted my ass for suddenly cut me and two hundred others loose in the middle of a recession. A high-paying middle management job with a promising future went right down the toilet. Welcome to the '90s. But, as I eventually found out, sometimes a recession ain't *all* bad.

Two months after I got the boot, I still had dick-all for a job. Sometimes it's not good having an MBA. There are either no jobs or you're overqualified for what's available. My Uncle Dave, who owns a big construction company in town, saw my frustration and tactfully offered me a job as a laborer to keep me going. I knew if I wanted to keep up the mortgage payments on my house I had to swallow my pride and take it. His only words of advice were, "Keep the gay thing to yourself, Greg. The men are pretty conservative. If they find out you're gay, you'll end up with more grief than you can handle."

Hey, I'm a realist. The last thing I need is grief. Besides, not being mechanical, I was more worried about handling a hammer than a homophobe.

The very next day, I was out at a site in the boonies, where a crew of about twenty guys was building a small strip mall. After the civility of an office environment, I felt like I had stepped onto another planet. The guys were all gruff, no-nonsense, blue-collar types. They ranged in age from early twenties to late fifties and came in a variety of shapes, sizes and ethnic backgrounds. Although skilled in their own particular trades, none struck me as being intellectually deep. For most of them, life was pretty basic and revolved around work, football, cars and finding a fuck or griping about the old lady. A guy pulled his weight and was respected or he was out. And I mean out fast. It was all very primal and macho. The simplicity appealed to me right from the beginning. And yes, they were conservative. Calling someone a faggot was the absolute worst slur these guys could throw.

It took a couple of weeks of back-breaking work before I earned enough respect to merit anything more than a casual greeting or cursory conversation. I was a non-skilled laborer at the bottom of the seniority pile, the lowest of the low, so I got every stinking shit-job that came along. And once word got out that I was the owner's nephew and had a degree, well, the guys went out of their way to find me the crud work. I considered quitting a million times, but always thought better of it. I needed the money and, okay, I admit it, I was lusting after the hottest fucking man I have ever seen in my life. A big hulking muscle-stud by the name of Bruno Manetti.

Not exactly drop-dead gorgeous in the looks department, Bruno is nonetheless a very striking, masculine, strong-featured hunk of man. In his early thirties, he's a stocky, olive-skinned Italian with curly black hair and dark brown eyes. After years of working construction by day and pumping iron by night, Bruno tips the scales at a jaw-dropping two hundred and forty pounds of power-packed meat. Everything about him is oversized and overdeveloped. He really has to be seen to be believed. Let me tell you, after seeing him once, I wanted him, and bad!

I was real careful around him but he understood right from the beginning that I was impressed by his size and appearance. Didn't bother him a bit. In fact, because I was discreet and didn't come on to him, I think the big lug got off on having an on-site fan club. I knew from years of first-hand experience at various gyms that guys into the muscle scene enjoy showing off what they've worked hard to achieve. They like to be admired and respected and really don't care who provides the attention.

So it was with Bruno. He still treated me like dirt around the other guys, but the T-shirts got smaller and the jeans went skin-tight so he could show off his big-gun arms, massive pecs, rippling abdominals, hefty basket, beautiful bubblebutt and tree-trunk thighs. As the days wore on, I also noticed that, whenever we were alone, he'd touch himself a lot. He would massage, stretch and flex those big muscles of his in a blatant display of masculine merchandising. Not only that, but he seemed to be kneading his crotch a lot more. Fuck, sometimes I can be so stupid.

It wasn't until we both happened to be taking a leak out behind a row of trucks that I clued in. Unlike the other guys, Bruno didn't turn away when he unzipped and hauled out his hefty chunk of uncut dick. In fact, he made a point of positioning himself so I had no problem seeing every inch of his mouth-watering manhood. He let loose with a stream of piss heavy enough to hose down a burning barn, which made him even more of a brute. I loved it.

I finished pissing. He finished pissing. Neither of us moved. I stood there staring at his cock. He stood there, big, meaty dick in hand, watching me stare at his cock. I broke out in a sweat, the tension was getting to me so bad. Then he started tugging on his dick. Tugging it and stretching it and gently shaking it from side to side. It didn't take long before the hooded, one-eyed phallus roused itself from rest and grew to monstrous, even frightening proportions. Simply put, he was hung like a horse!

"Holy fuck," I whimpered.

He liked that and started in right off with a serious stroking action. No nice and easy stuff for him. No fucking way. He wrapped that big paw-like hand of his around his big dick and pounded away like there was no tomorrow. Just kept going harder and faster, harder and faster until—*boom!* He let out a deep guttural groan like he just took a fist to the gut and the big, creamy cumwads started spurting out and splattering against the cab of the nearest pickup truck. Bam! Bam! Bam! What a load. Sure impressed me all to hell, and I've seen some big loads over the years! You'd have thought Bruno had been saving up for a couple of weeks.

It was too bad Bruno had to shoot and run. He'd barely squeezed out the last drop when he heard his name being called from where the Laundromat was going in. He snarled a frustrated, "Damn," and wrestled his cock back into his pants. "Gotta go," he grumbled and took off.

Yeah, sure, leave me hanging. I had to jack off too before going back to work, otherwise I'd never have gotten my hard-on back into my pants. As it was, I still went around all day sporting a woody. Damned embarrassing.

Next day, Bruno and I spent a hell of a lot of time hungrily eyeing each other but, what with one damned thing or another, we never got any time alone. I don't know about Bruno, but the situation drove me fucking crazy. Watching those big, hard, pumped muscles writhe, ripple and flex under that tight, sweat-soaked T-shirt was bad enough, but drooling all day over that big meaty schlong packed away between his legs, and not being able to lavish my considerable attention on it, was nothing short of cruel and unusual punishment.

Fortunately, I got my chance the following day. It was a Friday, and a payday to boot, so everyone was in a real good mood. Me, I was wired to the max and horny as hell. Anyway, there we were during lunch, sitting by the trucks, joking around and taking it easy, when the topic of work-related injuries came up. This naturally led to some of the guys showing off some of the grossest, nastiest-looking scars imaginable. This in turn led to a proud display of double-jointed body parts and other weird phenomena. Just as things were getting really rank, Bruno walked in on the gathering after finishing a report for head office. The guys thought this was perfect timing and a call went up.

"Show us your trick!" they all demanded. "Show us your trick!"

"What the fuck do you think I am?" Bruno shot back. "A trained fucking seal?"

His attitude didn't change until someone shouted, "Come on, Bruno, the new guy hasn't seen it."

That did it. Looking me right in the eye, he peeled off his tight T-shirt to reveal an incredible expanse of hairless, heavily muscled torso and said, "Then I guess I'd better show him."

The older, married guy next to me leaned close and mumbled, "Watch this, it'll turn your stomach."

Hell, just seeing the massive slabs of Bruno's bulging curved pecs with their quarter-sized aureole and thimble-sized nipples out in the open had not only set my stomach churning, but had given me the mother of all aching hard-ons. It was hard to imagine anything getting better than this.

Amid whoops and hollers, Bruno got a couple pairs of pliers out. Using elastic bands around their handles to keep them shut, he attached one to each of his thick, protruding nipples. Once they were clamped securely in place, he went through an impressive pec-posing routine to show how much pain a serious muscle-stud could take.

"Fuck, that's gotta hurt," whispered the older, married man. "And check it out! He's getting a hard-on. He must be getting off on it," he snorted. "That's just fuckin' sick."

Good thing the man didn't check my crotch or he'd have gotten doubly sick. Watching those pliers dangle from Bruno's big juicy man-tits while he flexed those monster pecs made my blood pressure skyrocket and my rock-hard dick cry out for release. Hell, I had a major wetstain just from the pre-cum.

After a couple of minutes of his crowd-pleasing routine, Bruno took off the pliers, rubbed his reddened nipples to get the circulation back and promptly announced he had to go take a leak. Off he went, a major boner straining against the confines of his pants, heading not to a nearby portable john but toward a large stand of trees way out of view at the far end of the site. I gave him about a minute, then mumbled loud enough so all could hear that I needed to take a leak. Off I went in hot pursuit, heart pounding, cock throbbing, not at all sure of the reception I was going to get but damned eager to find out.

When I finally found Bruno, he was leaning up against a tree, his pants down around his ankles, already going at it hot and heavy. His right hand was pounding the shit out of his hard cock while his left hand was going back and forth, making mincemeat out of his nipples.

"Here, let me do that," I said, brazenly walking right up to him. I latched onto those big beautiful nubs and gave them a good twist. His head dropped back, he let out a satisfied moan and started in on his cock double-time.

I can't tell you how much I love working a hot man's hot nips. Bruno's are fucking wonderful. Apart from being outrageously big, thick and rubbery, they are most definitely hooked directly to his overactive libido. Play with them a little and you rev his engine. Play with them a lot and you've got a wildman on your hands. He just couldn't get enough serious, soul-searching tit-play. He kept telling me to do it harder. He said he wanted to feel it, really feel it while I nearly ripped his bloated nubbly tits right off his chest! I was only too happy to oblige. Yessiree, big, beautiful, plump, super-sensitive man-sized tits.

We were both getting overheated incredibly fast. Considering this was neither the time nor the place for it, I decided to pull out the stops and send Bruno over the finish line in a big way. I dropped to my knees and, while still doing an expert number on his tits, took a deep breath and pounced on his fat uncut schlong.

There is nothing like the feel of a big uncut cock in your mouth to make you go apeshit. Bruno's got a real beauty: a huge, bulbous cockhead mounted on an enormous, thick, rock-solid shaft covered by a velvety-smooth sheath of slip-sliding foreskin. Beautiful, absolutely beautiful. And a real mouthful! Damn-near gagged me every time I got it all the way in, and I consider myself a cock-sucking expert! And did I mention his balls? They're big, heavy bull nuts dangling in a pliable, low-slung sac. You get those babies slapped across your face and you feel it! It makes you come alive, let me tell you.

Anyway, Bruno must have been primed and ready to go because all he needed was a couple of minutes of my hot, manipulative mouth on his throbbing cock to trigger his detonator. I felt his body shudder once, twice. He let out a muffled groan and—*boom!*—he had an orgasm like you would not believe!

I hung onto his tits for dear life and kept my mouth clamped tight onto his engorged, cum-spewing cock. Bruno's whole body jerked and spasmed like a gigantic rag doll above me. It was like a volcano going off! He just kept jerking that enormous body back and forth, flexing and relaxing those big muscles in a primal sex fit, nearly gagging me with all the thick creamy spunk that kept gushing out of his swollen dick. Had to swallow like crazy or I would have drowned in the stuff.

I kept suckin' on that fat dick until I made sure I'd squeezed every last drop of delicious, salty cum from every beautiful inch. It was only when I felt his hands under my arms that I let him out of my mouth and got to my feet. We stared into each other's eyes until Bruno finally broke the silence and said, "You are so fuckin' hot."

"Me? You 're the one who's a fuckin' fireball. Just stand there a minute and let me jack off," I replied, ripping open my pants and hauling out my hard meat. Since I honestly didn't expect him to reciprocate, I couldn't think of a more sincere compliment to pay him than jacking off over his mind-blowing masculinity.

"No. No fuckin' way. You're not going to waste a load like that when you got me so fuckin' horny," he said. Pulling a condom and a small tube of lube from his back pant pocket, he handed them to me and said, "Put this on and then fuck me. Fuck my ass good and hard. Right here, right now. Do it so hard that you fuck the ever lovin' shit out of me." With that he turned around, bent over, grabbed the tree for support and offered up the cute little pink puckered rosebud winking at me from between the twin globes of his curved muscular bubblebutt. One look at that magnificent upturned ass and I didn't need to be told twice. On went the condom, the lube, and in no time I was pulling up to the portal.

It took me a few moments to pop the tightened sphincter, but once I got my cockhead in, I took a deep breath and, knowing it was what Bruno wanted, rammed my rubberized dipstick in all the way to the balls in one hard, deep thrust. Bruno let out a satisfied groan and I knew I'd hit the bull's eye. From then on it was just a mindless crazed orgy of heavy duty, heat-stopping, gut-busting butt-fucking. None of that loving, tender, take-it-easy crap this time around. Bruno wanted it rough and I was just the man in just the mood to give it to him. He had to hang onto that tree for dear life, moaning and groaning the whole time, the way I shagged his ass.

Bruno's hot hole was so tight it was like a clamp on my dick. I pounded in and out of that chute like a piston from hell. Each hard, concentrated thrust brought a loud grunt from Bruno and bumped my balls one notch closer to the red zone, until suddenly the sizzling jizz in my percolating nuts hit its flashpoint and my cock took off with a life of its own. I buried my dick deep in Bruno's ass and held on tight while my balls exploded and emptied a heavy load of churning, burning cum into the latex love glove. It was one of the most intense orgasms I've ever had.

I had barely pulled out of that steaming ass when Bruno stood erect, took his rock-hard, cum-dripping uncut cock in hand and, after no more than ten or twelve serious strokes, came a second time, spattering the tree and surrounding underbrush with loads of his thick jism. I swear, the man's a cream machine! It was wild, fucking wild, how much came out. I almost gave a whoop of joy, it was so incredibly wild.

He milked his cock a couple of times, squeezing out every last creamy drop, then turned to me and said, "We better get back before they send out a search party." I reluctantly agreed and got down to the business of making myself presentable. Bruno did the same. I was just about to go when he held me by the wrist and said, "You doing anything tonight after work?"

"Didn't have any plans," I replied.

"Good. What say we grab something to eat, then go back to my place and grab each other?" he asked.

Direct and to the point. I like that in a man. And that's what we did. Grab, grab, grab. All weekend long. From then on we were buddies and, as the saying goes, the rest is history.

A year later, we're still buddies. And the sex is as hot and sweaty as ever. Bruno moved in with me not long after that wild weekend. A month after that, we quit my uncle's company to form our own small outfit. We got tired of the bullshit once word got out just how buddy-buddy we had become. Most of the guys simply could not handle the situation.

It turned out for the best, though. Bruno is finally his own boss and I do the paper work. Times are tight, what with the economy and all, but we're doing okay. Next time you need some work done, give us a call. Buddies Construction. We'll get the job done right. Guaranteed.

Catalyst

IT WAS PAST MIDNIGHT when the Harley pulled up in front of the seedy roadside bar. "This looks like a good spot," Rick said, kicking out the stand.

From his seat behind the driver's broad, leather-clad back, Steve looked at the dive and the other half-dozen mudcaked choppers parked to one side of it. What a hole, he thought. He could just imagine who—or what—lay inside. But if Rick said a spot was good, then who was he to argue? "Can't be any worse than that bare-knuckle boxing card he dragged me to last month," he muttered under his breath.

Steve accepted that Rick "The Prick" Mancini had to work off his pent-up anger and frustration somehow (the pressure that builds within a big-city cop being what it is, and all that shit). And he accepted that Rick had an insatiable, near-demonic libido that kept him at a sexual fever-pitch even on his "slow days." But fuck, this intense high-risk search of his for the ultimate in kink adventure was putting a severe strain on his nerves. Especially since it seemed the riskier and more dangerous the adventure, the more eagerly Rick embraced it. Where was it all going to end? Would the man and his libido ever be satisfied?

Inside the bar, Steve's eyes widened in surprise. Holy fuck. He couldn't believe it, the place was a veritable Coney Island of raunch and debauchery! Old neon beer signs and dinky red-shaded overheads cast surreal pools of flickering, nether-world light in the otherwise pitch-black den of iniquity. Heavy clouds of stale cigar smoke hung in the air almost, but not quite, overpowering the gut-wrenching stench of sweat, piss, amyl and fresh vomit. The Rolling Stones' "You Can't Always Get What You Want" blasted out at something like 140 decibels, numbing the brain and providing a raucous musical backdrop for the action within.

Scattered about the room, grunting and heaving like a pack of rutting animals, five bikers (ranging from fat and pig-ugly to lean, hot and humpy) were getting their rocks off in a variety of ways with an equal number of bruised, battered and buck naked local boys. If not getting exactly what they wanted, the bikers were sure as hell getting what they appeared to need.

His eyes glowing like hot coals, Mancini leaned close and chortled in Steve's ear, "Fuck, a scene can't get much better than this!"

"Yeh, sure," Steve mumbled, noting with disgust that none of the locals could exactly be called consenting.

One was lashed face-down over the side of a pool table getting brutally fucked by Greaser, a paunchy ex-jock in a greasy Elvis-style pompadour. Another was strung up to an overhead water-pipe, toes barely touching the floor, while a short, lean, weasel-like little motherfucker beat his ass raw with the narrow end of a pool cue. Another was on his belly licking the dirty boots of a big hairy bear of a man, who was laughing his head off as he pissed all over the trembling supplicant. A skinny kid barely out of his teens was on his knees blowing an immense, tattooed, scowling Buddha, who sat spread-legged on a chair puffing a fat cigar and playing with the doorknocker-sized rings hanging from his humongous, sagging tits. Yet another kid was eating out the ass of a Tom of Finland-type biker, a strikingly handsome stud with huge defined muscles and a gigantic cut cock, who seemed more interested in the old pinball machine he was playing than the quality of the rim job.

"What'd I tell you," smirked Mancini. "Is this a good spot, or what?"

Steve didn't get a chance to reply. Just when his gut instinct was telling him something wasn't right, Mick and The Stones went dead and the click of a revolver being cocked behind him cut through the sudden silence. That's when he realized what was bugging him. He had counted five guys getting serviced but there were six choppers outside!

The bikers tossed their playmates aside like so many discarded toys and quickly formed a menacing semi-circle around the interlopers. There was an uncomfortable, interminable silence while everyone sized everyone else up until, finally, Mancini drawled, "Is this a private party or can anyone join in?"

The psycho holding the gun nervously licked his lips and stroked his long, skinny dick a couple of times. "Man, you and your buddy look like a couple of alright dudes. We insist you stay. In fact, you're gonna be the guests of honor. Right, guys?"

"Right."

"Right."

"Yeh, right."

"So, strip, let's see your party favors, and then we're gonna get down and have us some serious fun. Know what I mean?"

Shrugging out of his black leather jacket, Mancini looked at Steve and deadpanned, "Sounds good to me. I'm all for Serious Fun."

"Right," Steve agreed, apprehensively. "Serious fun."

So, under the hostile, demented eye of the gun-toting Psycho, they stripped. Once naked, the bikers made a big deal out of poking and prodding them, pulling on this and squeezing that until, despite his growing hard-on, Mancini suddenly got belligerent and shoved back.

Without warning, Tommy spun around and caught Mancini in the crotch with his knee. The unexpected blow was too much, even for the big, thrill-seeking cop. His face went white and, clutching his battered balls, he dropped to the floor gasping for breath and groaning in agony.

Blooded, the bikers set on Mancini like a pack of hungry wolves. First they tried kicking the shit out of him, stopping only long enough to allow the burly hairy one, Bear, to yank Mancini's arms behind his back and tie his wrists together with some rope so that they could open up again on his unprotected mid-section. That lasted until Mancini started dry-heaving (good thing he hadn't eaten since lunch).

Then Buddha latched onto Mancini's monster nips and used the nubs to drag him to a chair, where he really did a number on them. There was no finesse, no style. Buddha was so brutal to those pec-nobs even Steve got squeamish. Stayed squeamish, too, right up until Mancini let out an animal roar and shot a heavy load all over Buddha's sagging blubbergut.

Enraged that Mancini would get off under such harsh treatment, the bikers warmed his face with the backs of their hands, then dragged him over to the pool table where they shoved him face down on the green baize and tanned his ass with their wide leather belts. They kept that up until their arms got tired and his asscheeks glowed.

Then they fucked him. A couple of them twice. Except for Psycho, of course, who held onto the gun and pounded his pud. They all took great pleasure in the notion they were destroying a massive specimen of manhood by violating the hot musclestud's unwilling ass with their macho, straight dicks. At least, by the way he was struggling, they assumed the musclestud felt the sanctity of his manhood was being violated.

Ah, if they only knew, sneered Steve. He was concerned at what Mancini was enduring physically, yet understood the well from which the man's inner needs sprang. Sometimes, he reasoned, inner needs demanded violation. And being violated didn't necessarily mean losing control of the situation, either. An interesting contradiction in terms, he acknowledged, one it was probably better the bikers didn't know about. The dumb fucks.

The bikers were gentler with Steve. Maybe because they were tired after their workout with Mancini, maybe because Steve was more cooperative. In any case, once their biggest problem was safely strung up and effectively out of the way, they could afford to take their time, relax and enjoy themselves. They still worked Steve over good but gone was the malice they had used on Mancini. And, to Steve's great relief, they didn't do a number on his face. That counted for a lot.

It helped that Steve clued in real fast to each biker's particular turn-on and punched the right buttons to show them all a good time. Compared with the hardcore sexstuds he was used to, the bikers were babes in the woods. Simple men with simple kinks. Still, being the consummate sexual gamesman and ingrained with a strong sense of duty and a deep-rooted desire to please, Steve never held back or gave anything less than 100%. Any job worth doing is a job worth doing well, he figured. Even if a gun to the head factored into the motivation.

Mostly, the action meant sucking, ball-licking and getting fucked. The basics. They all liked a good gut-churning blowjob to get them revved up and raging hard and then they'd push Steve over and plug his tight little ass.

In between the blowjob and the getting fucked each biker got off on his own little sidetrip. The Variations. Weasel warmed Steve's clenched buttcheeks with the palm of his broad, callused hand, delighting in the choked sobs and streaming tears he brought forth, before finally driving his dick home. Greaser got off on having his low-hanging balls and thick cheesy foreskin worked over, almost creaming himself when Steve made like a sewing machine with his teeth across his overhang. Bear was probably happier pissing on Steve's face after he shot his load than either before or during his orgasm—and, man, could he piss up a storm! Buddha needed his megatits tortured before he could cum (no surprise there). And Tommy? Fuck, Tommy liked nothing better than a good rimming. Like most athletes totally in tune with their bodies and possessing heightened physical responses, once Tommy got going he thoroughly enjoyed just about anything and everything Steve did to him. He was so responsive, in fact, that Steve didn't mind servicing him one bit. Nope, not one little fucking bit!

Better yet, on top of the fun Steve was having with the humpy biker, he detected more than a cursory interest on Mancini's part as to what he was doing. Was it even remotely possible Mancini might be jealous, he wondered? Was there a chance Mancini might be pissed off at not only being forced to watch him service another man but seeing how much he enjoyed doing so? That would be choice, snorted Steve, and perhaps the best revenge of all.

By the icy stare and clenched jaw, Steve could tell Mancini was feeling *something*. He redoubled his efforts on Tommy's sizable equipment and was rewarded with an earth-rumbling moan from Tommy and a view of Mancini's fiery black eyes narrowing into cold, murderous slits.

While he pounded Tommy's thick cock with one hand and yanked the man's low-hanging balls with the other, Steve licked his way up the stud's undulating abs to the heaving, muscle-laden chest. He slavishly tongued all the way around the defined edges of the slab-like pecs, then sucked on the small virgin-smooth nipples until they hardened and he could get his teeth on them.

But Tommy was a tit-novice and it didn't take much before he let out a howl and jerked back. "Owww! Hey, watch it! That fuckin' hurt!"

"I'm sorry, Sir, very sorry," apologized Steve. He glanced over at Mancini, at the bloated monster tits on the man's chest and cracked a thinly-veiled smile, knowing that Mancini's nips yearned for exactly what Tommy had rejected. "I guess I got carried away, Sir," he whimpered, before lapping at the offended nipple, hoping to make amends. Hoping to antagonize Mancini further.

"Yeah, that's better. I don't like any of that pain shit."

Too bad, thought Steve, you don't know what you're missing. He winked at Mancini, as if to say, "But you do," then dropped to his knees and went back to work on Tommy's cock.

"Yeah, suck that cock. Suck my big man's cock. That's right, take it all the way. All the way. Choke on it, yeah, I want to see you fuckin' choke on it. Awwfuck, that feels good. You like that? You like suckin' my big fuckin' piece of meat?"

"Yes, Sir," Steve gasped, "I like it very much. It's so hot, so fuckin' hot. A real man's cock. A real fuck—"

"Shut up and work my balls. I want you to work on my balls now. Yeah, that's it. Lick 'em, lick 'em good. Really get down and lick 'em. Yeh, now suck 'em into your mouth. Yeah, that's it. Good boy. Suck on 'em, suck on 'em like you mean it. Yeah, that's it. Ohhhfuuuuck, that feels good. That feels so. . . . Just a second, just a second. Let go. Let go! You got me so fuckin' horny, I want your tongue up my ass. I want you eatin' out my ass."

While Tommy was busy turning around, Steve checked on Mancini and was jolted by one of the most impressive sights of his life. The cop was glaring at him with everything from pain and indignation to hate and disgust ablaze in his eyes. Every muscle on his massive 6′1″, 240-pound frame was tensed in awesome, gut-wrenching relief as he strained against the ropes binding his wrists to the overhead pipe. He wanted to fucking kill somebody, he was so riled!

But his cock, his cock was the most mind-blowing sight of all! Despite the incredible rage surging through his body—or maybe because of it—his ten fat inches were pumped to the max, aching for action. Ten big, fat inches of awesome, vein-popping, cum-dripping manmeat.

I think I got his attention, Steve acknowledged. He nervously buried himself in the crack of Tommy's muscular ass and gorged himself on the treasure within, satisfied he was not only making one hot man very happy but successfully mindfucking another.

"Ohhfuuuuuuuuck, yesss!" groaned Tommy. Less than five minutes into his rimjob and he was on the brink of losing it. "Turn around! Get up and turn around, I said! I want to fuck you. I want to fuck you up the ass before I come. I want to fuckin' shoot my load up your ass! Hurry, before I lose it!"

Steve did as he was told, leaning on a table for support against the brutal rear-end assault. The fuck was a heart-stopper but the real icing on the cake was facing Mancini while it happened. The frustration and impotent rage on Mancini's face at Steve's perceived insubordination was worth every bone-jarring thrust. To twist the knife further, Steve went all out with his moaning and groaning (not that he wasn't having a good time anyway), figuring that the extra audio was sure to get under the cop's skin. There'd be hell to pay for it later, he knew, but it would be well worth it. Two could play at this game.

"Oh, yeah, Sir, fuck my ass. *Fuck* my ass good and hard. Fuck me harder! HARDER! Yeah, ram it in! Shove it, really *shove* it in! Shove your big fuckin' meat all the way! Hurt me! Hurt me, I can take it! Fuck me! *Fuck me*! AHHHHH!"

"Aww! Awwshit! Aww! Ohhhfuuuck, YES! I—Ahhhhhhhhhh!" Spent, Tommy pulled out and slumped down in the nearest chair. "Oh, yeah," he sighed happily.

Steve smirked over at Mancini as if to say, "How do you like them apples?" But his gloating was cut short by Weasel, who came out of nowhere, grabbed him by the scruff of his neck and forced him to his knees.

"Open up, faggot. Suck me off," he barked, ramming his dinky hard-on into Steve's mouth. "You like cock so much, show me again how much you like this one!"

Steve did his best. The guy was slime and didn't interest—much less excite—him in the least. But Steve had too much pride to turn in a bad performance so, battling mind-numbing boredom and scum-induced nausea, he gave the little runt the blowjob of his life. It was the stuff of Purple Hearts.

But instead of a medal all he got for his efforts—one of the best performances of his cocksucking career—was a shudder and a single, tiny little squirt. Terrific.

He gave the dwindling weenie one last, methodical milking and let it slip unceremoniously from between his tingling lips. That was pretty pathetic, he thought, swallowing the meager results of his labors. He looked up from his kneeling position and asked respectfully, "Will that be all, Sir?"

"Yeah, I guess so," Weasel snorted. Then he swaggered off to get a beer. But not before he sent Steve sprawling with a shove of his foot, just for the hell of it.

"Thank you, Sir," mumbled Steve, gingerly getting back up on his knees. Thank you so very fucking much. Asshole.

Psycho was standing over by the pool table, watching him with a gun in one hand and his pud in the other. It was a wonder he hadn't rubbed himself raw, the way he'd been going at it. Still hadn't cum, either. Weird. I wonder what it takes to get him off, Steve mused. Not that he really cared. He was too tired, sore and worn out for that.

Fuck, he reckoned even Mancini hadn't fully expected the kind of treatment they ended up getting from the six Bikers From Hell. He looked over at the muscled brute and, like always, even after all they'd been through, felt his gut churn and his cock harden. He cursed the man for still having an effect on him even after all they'd been through. He was tired of the games, tired of the shit he had to endure for the man. A man who held him in so little regard.

Steve staggered to his feet and stumbled over to the trussed cop. Mancini was hanging by his rope-bound wrists from an overhead pipe like a side of beef, his toes barely scraping the linoleum floor, his beefy body showing the effects of a thorough working over.

His face was a mess. His right eye was almost swollen shut, it was so beat-up. Welts, cuts and lacerations marked him all over below the neck, especially across the shoulders, back, ass and abs. His nipples were inflamed to incredible cow-teat proportions. His gargantuan dick and bull balls were hanging low and glowing bright red. Cum dribbled down the inside of his legs from an asshole too tired to contain it. Yeah, he'd been worked over good. Real good.

"You bastard," Steve snarled, his wavering voice filled with scorn and disdain. "See what trying to satisfy your fucking needs has done to us?"

"What the fuck's going on here?" It was Psycho, nervously waving the gun in Steve's face. His other hand was still on his hard cock, still pounding away.

"Shut up," Steve snapped, "this is between him and me!" He spat at the cop but derived only the slightest gratification. Digging his thumbnails into the bloated, tenderized tits made him feel no better, either.

"What's the matter," taunted Mancini, "do my needs scare you?"

"I accept the fact you have needs," Steve hissed back. "I get off on most of them myself. I'm just wondering where the fuck it's all going to end."

"Get away from him!" Psycho was freaking.

"What's it going to take to finally make you happy, Mancini?"

"Fuck if I know."

"Damn you!" Out of sheer frustration Steve hauled off and slugged the monster cop in the gut.

Mancini let out a roar and every muscle in his body instinctively contracted against the pain. But bound as he was to the pipe, with his arms trussed above his head and his legs straining to take the weight off his wrists, his movement was so restricted as to be useless. His size and conditioning counted for diddly-squat as long as his vitals remained exposed and unprotected. The impotence—or was it fear?—reflected in his eyes confirmed the fact.

Psycho stepped in to grab Steve's arm and pull him away. "I said—" he shouted, but that's all he got out. Mancini's foot lashed out in a perfectly-executed karate kick and connected with the base of his neck, whipping his head back with a sickening "crack" and dropping him in his tracks. Probably never knew what hit him.

Mancini gave a blood-curdling yell and snapped the rope binding his wrists like so much cheap twine. He hit the ground running and went straight for Tommy, who was pulverized with a series of lightning-fast bodyblows before getting dropped by a wicked roundhouse kick to the head.

It didn't take long for the last four bikers to meet much the same fate. They tried fighting back but their bare hands were no match against Mancini's unrelenting size, strength and martial arts skills. Not to mention the anger and thirst for revenge fuelling his attack.

It wasn't pretty. Bear collapsed in a corner puking his guts out after a vicious knee to the nuts. Greaser had something in his leg snap because of a devastating mulekick. Weasel got pitched headfirst into a wall. And Buddha had his head used as a punching bag. Four up, four down.

Mancini stood in the center of the bar and surveyed the mayhem around him. Six biker scum out of commission with varying degrees of damage. Some of it quite possibly permanent. Too bad, too fucking bad, said the sneer on his face.

Satisfied with his handiwork, Mancini stashed the gun in his jacket, then focused his attention on Steve. His eyes were cold, his face devoid of expression. "Time to mop up," he intoned.

An icy chill ran up Steve's spine. "What . . . what do you mean?"

Mancini wrapped a big paw around his thick hunk of meat and stroked its monstrous proportions. "I mean . . ." he growled, "turn around and bend over."

Steve took a fearful step back. "Please, I . . ."

Mancini's deliberate advance left no doubt as to his intentions. "You'll save yourself a lot of grief if you give me what I want."

"No, I . . . I don't want to. Please. Please, Sir, don't."

"Don't? You're saying 'don't' to me? Me? After what I saw you do with them?"

"I—" Panic-stricken, Steve made a sudden, last-ditch dash, hoping to fake the cop out and put some space between them.

No such luck, It was as if Mancini had read his mind. Steve deeked right into the man's waiting arms. He barely had time to let out a choked yelp before getting flipped over and slam-dunked onto the pool table. His head bounced once and that was it. Game over.

When he came to his senses a few moments later he was flat on his back with his legs in the air and his ass hanging over the pool table's edge. Mancini was looming over him, holding him down with his hands while his angry red fuckpole pressed insistently against his trembling, resistant asshole.

"No, Sir! Please, no," Steve sobbed. "I don't—"

"You don't *nothing*!" hissed Mancini. "You got that, mister? You're mine. My property. And that means I can do anything I want to you!"

"Yes, Sir. I know, Sir. But it's gotta be—"

"It's gotta be nothing. *Nothing*!"

"Oh God, I'm sorry for what I—"

"Sorry? It's too fucking late for that, shithead. I'll give you something to feel sorry about."

"I was wrong, Sir. I accept. . . . Sir, you can't do it this way. We have to both . . . It's gotta be . . ."

One mighty shove and Mancini rammed his shaft in to the hilt, ending the discussion. Steve let out an agonized scream as the pain radiated from his ass.

The fuck that followed was hard and brutal, totally devoid of any tenderness or consideration. If anything, Mancini went out of his way to be excessively cruel. Steve's hole wasn't exactly tight from the earlier biker workouts but it was still totally unprepared for the furious mind-numbing assault. In more ways than one it was the hardest fuck of Steve's entire life.

"AAAAAAAAAAAAAAAAHHHH!"

The look on Mancini's face as he squeezed the last drop of jizz from his softening dick was one of pure satisfaction. "Mmmm, I needed that," he sighed. "Okay, time to get dressed. The show's over and we've got a long ride ahead of us."

"Yes, Sir. Anything you say, Sir."

Must have been the hollow, distant way Steve said it. Mancini turned and looked him square in the eye. "I'm a conceited, arrogant prick with a major attitude problem. I treat you like shit and don't give you the respect you deserve. But rest assured, in my own way, I love you. Only you."

"I . . . I know, Sir," Steve replied. "I appreciate you telling me, though. Thank you."

"Alright then. Now, let's cut the sentimental crap and haul ass. Oh, and if you ever look like you enjoy getting fucked by another man again, I'll really show you a thing or two."

Tsunami

KENZO FUKUDA STUCK his head in Randy's office and with a big shit-eating grin on his face asked, "Hey, hotshot, how'd you like to check out some sweaty fat men?"

Randy froze, caught totally off-guard by the bizarre proposition. Kenzo was a real wild and crazy guy, a corporate samurai with a quick wit and wicked sense of humor. Randy knew from personal experience that given Kenzo's capabilities anything was possible. "Sweaty fat men?"

"I'm talking sumo. You know, the big fat guys who wrestle. The company's a corporate sponsor for one of the biggest stables in Tokyo."

"Stables?"

"Yeah, heya. That's what you call a bunch of sumotori. They're like clubs or dojos. Anyway, Mr. Hashimoto thought you might like to see one. Kind of a reward for all the long hours you're putting in. I think he likes you. Hey, it's a big honor. Not many gaijin get to hang out with rikishi. Come on."

"Whoa, Kenzo-san," sputtered Randy, glancing helplessly at the stack of papers on his desk. He enjoyed working in Japan but didn't think he'd ever get used to the insane pace. "It's only nine-thirty. We haven't even had our morning coffee yet."

"No time for coffee. Most sumotori start training at 5:00 a.m. and finish at eleven. We're late already. Come on, Mr. Hashimoto's orders. He say take the day off and show Randy a good time."

How could Randy argue with that? He was pleased his boss liked the job he was doing but he didn't think hanging out with a bunch of sumo wrestlers would be his idea of fun. Still, don't look a gift horse in the mouth, he reminded himself.

Once at the stable's keiko-ba, or practice area, he was introduced to the stablemaster (a retired Grand Champion) and then to the 30-odd sumotori. Most of the sumotori (also called rikishi) were beginner or middle-ranked wrestlers but there was a smattering of high-ranked sumotori as well as one yokozuna, or Grand Champion. Almost all of the middle and high-ranked sumotori were large, grossly overweight men but even the beginners were well on their way to the enormous, ponderous size and shape most rikishi are noted for.

Randy stood at the back of the practice area and watched the proceedings with a bewildering mixture of rapt fascination and perverse, gut-churning desire. For someone who thought he was attracted only to the buffed, tanned bodies of the trendy gym-toned Muscle Beach crowd, he couldn't believe how turned on he was by all this portly Tokyo pulchritude. Maybe it was because everyone was so large and physically awe-inspiring. Maybe it was the heady ultra-masculine venue reeking of rampant testosterone. Or maybe it was because the only thing the men wore was a thick cotton belt-cum-loincloth, a mawashi, around their waists which barely covered their groin and the crack of their ass and left the rest of their large beefy bodies exposed and on display for all to see. Whatever the reason, the sizzle in Randy's pants told him something was happening.

Two hulking, sweat-drenched behemoths lumbered to the center of the ring and hunkered down into a three-point stance eager to do battle. At over 350 pounds apiece—most of it pure unadulterated fat—they were in their physical prime and at the peak of their profession. They had it all: enormous weight, imposing girth, formidable strength, the brazen self-confidence that comes from years of hard-won experience and (perhaps most important of all) a low, practically immovable center of gravity. One couldn't help but be impressed.

There was a brief, tension-packed pause and then, with an explosive bellow, the two humongous gladiators suddenly sprang up and hurled themselves at each other with all their might. After the initial impact there followed a fast and furious, rough and ready pushing and shoving match which, surprisingly enough, couldn't have lasted more than thirty seconds. The match ended abruptly when the slightly smaller of the two combatants got a good grip on the larger's mawashi and, using it for leverage, managed to hip-toss the larger man to the packed-clay floor.

"Alright, way to go!" exclaimed Randy. He quickly recovered his composure, mumbled, "I can't believe I'm getting into this," and glanced about the room hoping no one had noticed. That's when he locked eyes—yet again—with the arresting, heart-stopping hunk in the deep purple mawashi on the other side of the keiko-ba.

The big, sexy stud was a handsome, strapping lad of about twenty-five who stood close to six feet tall and weighed in the neighborhood of 300 pounds. While undeniably smooth and chunky, he also had the solid, densely-muscled foundation that comes from lifting a hell of a lot of heavy weights so that, unlike most of the other sumotori who resembled large overweight Buddhas, he was built more along the lines of a bulky powerlifter gone soft. His squared, heavy-set shoulders were barn-door wide and incredibly thick; his massive pecs, decorated with their two eye-catching, silver dollar-sized nipples, were curved slabs sagging under their own weight; his huge, corded arms, with biceps that bulged to the size of small cannonballs, were obviously power-packed and not just for show; his tree-trunk thighs and ham-sized calves bespoke legs that could move small mountains. Yeah, he was built, alright.

He had a prominent, overhanging gut but even from a distance it, too, appeared solid as a rock and very appealing. On him it looked good, damn good, and it (along with everything else about the man) set Randy's insides churning something fierce.

Randy nudged Kenzo on the sly and whispered, "Who's that?"

"Who? Him? Oh, even I know that. Name's Tetsuro Morizaki, a real up and comer. One of sumo's New Breed. He's going to be a yokozuna in no time. His nickname's 'Tsunami' because he hits his opponents like a tidal wave and overwhelms them with his size and strength. Good looking guy, huh?"

"Yeah, he is," Randy admitted, hoping he wasn't giving anything away.

"Rumor has it," Kenzo continued, his voice barely audible, "that Tsunami is big, very big." He held his index fingers about seven inches apart to illustrate.

Randy smiled politely and replied with a suitably impressed, "Ah, so." He glanced over to find the hunky stud glaring daggers at him. Oops, someone's a little choked, he thought. A playful wink only seemed to make matters worse. Hmmm, I guess the big guy thinks I'm one to kiss and tell, he reckoned.

Not that Randy didn't have a lot to kiss and tell about. Who would have thought that the hot, responsive stranger he'd had the serious, heavy-duty encounter with just a few nights previous would turn out to be a famous, up and coming young sumotori? Hell, at the time, Randy took him for a rich, good-looking fat boy out to satisfy a few carnal cravings. Randy smiled at the irony and at the memory of that night. Turned out the fat boy was a pig, a real sex pig, and the encounter was one Randy would never forget.

The meeting had been arranged through trusted intermediaries after discreet inquiries were made regarding the availability of Randy's "special" services. It seems Randy's reputation for safe, sane, anything-goes kink and perversion had spread through the Tokyo sexual underground and had been picked up by "an important personage" who had a passion for pain and a need for anonymity. Despite his reluctance to make it with a total stranger, Randy finally agreed to a session once he'd been assured in no uncertain terms that the man would be more than worth it.

A fat boy, thought Randy, when he first laid eyes on the corpulent, casually-dressed young man who finally showed up at the small, well-equipped private dungeon that had been made available for their use. He ain't nothing but a big ol' Japanese fat boy.

Considering his last sex partner had been a former Mr. Japan, the ample dimensions of this new man totally threw Randy for a loop. He had real trouble reconciling the man's size with the "he's worth it" assurances. Yeah, right, suckered again, he groused. They bowed and without further ado Randy growled, "Okay, fat boy, strip."

Once he saw the man buck naked in all his beefy, muscular glory, however, Randy started having second thoughts about his "fat boy" put-downs and slowly came to a startling, somewhat unsettling conclusion: he was getting turned on by the guy. The hunk's imposing size, extravagant bulk and obvious masculinity were tripping a switch in his subconscious and doing a number between his legs. Hmmmm, he said, as he ran his hands over the enormous, sagging pecs and full, protruding gut before going lower and checking out the powerful, elephantine thighs and formidable, boxcar butt. Hmmmmm, indeed.

As previously agreed upon, the first nature of business was tying the man up. Yet another strong, well-built, macho-type stud gets off on relinquishing control of his body, his mind and his destiny, mused Randy, as he stretched the brawny, 300-pounder out in a wide, standing "X" between the two upright wooden posts. With the gentle, soothing sounds of taped koto music playing softly in the background, Randy spent the next hour skillfully constructing an intricate spider's web of knotted ropes between the two posts so that, by the time he was finished, the big man was securely imprisoned within the taut, expert weaving and rendered a complete and utterly immobile captive.

Next step: Randy applied his considerable expertise to the task of encasing the hefty hunk's entire body in a complex rope lattice work of large, diamond-shaped designs. No body part was spared. Arms, legs, torso, even the head, were bound. Randy wasn't delicate about it, either. The ropes went on so tight that the fat (especially in places like the gut, chest and thighs, where there was lots of it) bunched into angry little pillows of puffed-up, reddened flesh, which spilled out between the diamonds and gave the body an over-stuffed, quilted look.

As requested, the massive pecs and dangling bull balls received special consideration. Ropes wrapped around above and below the pecs (in addition to those cinched in a wide "X" across the chest), forced the huge beefy slabs into two immense, swollen mounds of monster-sized, mouth-watering mantit. The chunky stud ended up with bigger breasts than most women. And very impressive breasts they were, too. Below, rope wound neatly around the hairless ballsac forced the big bull nuts down low—very low—to the bottom of the sac while a loop around the base of the erect cock made the shaft swell to even more amazing, rock-hard proportions. Artistic and functional, it was a superior tie-off! Randy leaned in close and asked, "You okay, fat boy?"

"Yes, Sir. Thank you, Sir," panted the big guy.

"Good, because it gets better," replied Randy, who was by this time really getting into it.

Clothespins came next, lots of them. A couple of hundred, at least. They went on in a neat line up the inside of the bound man's legs, along the underside of his arms, up both sides of his torso, criss-crossed (twice) his big overhanging gut, went along the outer edges of his pecs and encircled his crotch.

The big man kept his mouth shut but, going by the sweat, his furrowed brow and tensed, trembling body, he was in sweet, delicious agony. He didn't crack until Randy attached the rubber-tipped, alligator-toothed clamps to his huge, engorged nipples and stuck a lubed, jumbo-sized buttplug up his tight ass. That's when he lost it and started writhing (as best he could) and moaning in uncontrollable pain which, of course, only encouraged Randy to redouble his efforts.

The hunky stud came three times that night. The first, when Randy was well into a heavy-duty flagellation scene with a wicked cat-o'-nine-tails, was a loud, raucous, gut-busting celebration of primal male release. The second, when Randy used the soft nylon bristles of an ordinary hair brush on his raging hard-on, was quieter but no less intense. And the third, despite his loud, repeated protests, came when Randy pulled out the buttplug and fucked his big ol' fat boy ass like a wild animal in heat. Number three was the most impressive of all.

Randy didn't ordinarily go against the express wishes of a sex partner but this time around he couldn't help himself. He was just too revved and over-excited to stop. It was a real thrill hanging onto the big, trussed-up side of manbeef and rubbing his hands all over those little pockets of flesh while the stud struggled beneath him. It was such a turn-on he ended up coming three times himself. Downright fucking amazing, he thought!

"I told you, I don't get fucked," snarled the big man, once he'd been released from his rope bonds at the end of the evening. He was too stiff, tired and tender at that point, though, to do much more than wave a thick, stubby finger in Randy's face.

"Well, you got fucked tonight, fat boy," Randy growled back. "And you know what? You fuckin' loved it!"

The look in the sexy, dark brown eyes told Randy the man was too proud to admit the truth. They glared at each other a long, long time until, feeling his cock stir again, Randy said, "It's time for you to go."

"Yes, Sir. Thank you, Sir." The stud bowed very deep and held the bow for a very long time. When he straightened up again he said quietly, "One day, Sir, I will repay the courtesy. I will fuck your hot little gaijin ass."

"Yeah, right. Don't hold your breath, fat boy," snorted Randy. "This hot little gaijin ass doesn't roll over for just anybody and, well, I can't imagine getting fucked by someone who's got his own zip code."

Randy couldn't get the harsh words out of his head. The longer he stared across the keiko-ba at the striking, heavy-set number he now knew as Tsunami, the more he regretted having said them. He wished there was some way he could make amends but, judging by how angrily the handsome hunk glared back at him, he figured the only acceptable apology would be ritual hara-kiri.

Practice ended shortly after eleven. By then the sumotori were tired, hungry and clearly in no mood to continue. All they wanted was a bath, lots of food and their afternoon nap. After a short pep-talk by the stablemaster they were wisely dismissed for the day. While the rikishi were packing it in, the stablemaster came over and asked his guests what they thought of the practice.

Kenzo's response was polite but it was obvious that sumo was not his cup of tea. Randy on the other hand, in his best albeit rudimentary Japanese, assured the stablemaster that he had had a great time and was now a confirmed fan. He mentioned that he had wrestled in college and joked that he was glad he never had to face any of this particular stable's fearsome rikishi.

"Why didn't you say you were a fellow wrestler?" boomed the stablemaster. "Once a wrestler, always a wrestler. I'll bet you've been itching for a match, just waiting for a chance to use all your old skills again. Wouldn't it be something to tell your family and friends back home in America!"

"I—you're too kind—but—" sputtered Randy.

"This is terrific," Kenzo whooped. "Randy the Rikishi! I can't wait to tell Mr. Hashimoto."

"Men, wait a minute," the stablemaster called out after the departing rikishi. "We have a fellow wrestler visiting us today. An American. He is very impressed with sumo and I think, out of courtesy, it would be most desirable if he left our heya with a match under his belt. Is there anyone here who would like the honor of competing against him?"

"Hai! Yes, I would!"

"Tsunami! Excellent! Come, meet our guest."

The stern, imposing rikishi strode over and the two men were formally introduced. At only 5′8″, 160 pounds, Randy was reminded how David must have felt going up against Goliath. His hand was swallowed whole when they shook and he couldn't help but feel puny, real puny standing there.

Tsunami was still gripping Randy's hand—a hard, bone-crushing grip it was, too—when he asked point-blank, "So, you think you've got what it takes to be a sumotori?"

Trying not to wince against the pain, Randy replied as pleasantly as he could, "You're obviously very big and strong, Tsunami-san, but I can take anything you can dish out. Anything at all. And who knows, I might even surprise you. My size and agility just might tie you up in knots."

The shallow, condescending smile melted off Tsunami's otherwise dour, sullen face. "We'll see about that," he snarled.

It was suggested that to protect his clothes and make him feel more like a sumotori Randy should strip down to his undershorts. At this point Randy was game for anything. Four times a week gym workouts gave him an impressive, muscular build with good size and great definition—quite different from Tsunami's combination of large, bulky muscle padded by an excess of chunky beef. This, coupled with the fact that Randy had a pale complexion, blond crewcut hair and blue eyes while Tsunami had long black hair (pulled back into a styled topknot), dark brown eyes and a light mahogany-hued skin tone (neither had body hair) made for an interesting contrast of masculine types.

Settling into his three-point stance in the center of the ring, Tsunami glared at Randy and, under his breath, snapped, "What the fuck are you doing here?"

"Whoa, ease up, fat boy. I'm just as surprised as you are," Randy snapped back. He hunkered down into position and then playfully added, "Geez, if I'd known you were going to be this grumpy I would have brought along some rope."

Tsunami shot Randy a deadly, withering look. His eyes narrowed to murderous slits and he growled, "Not funny."

The stablemaster gave a shout and Randy instantly sprang into action. Like he'd observed during practice, he hurled himself at Tsunami with all the force he could muster, hoping to throw the rikishi off balance or push him out of the ring in the opening seconds of the match. No such luck. Initially caught off-guard by the ferocity of Randy's attack, Tsunami staggered back a couple of steps but then, regaining his balance, planted his feet in a wide defensive stance and suddenly became all but immovable.

Randy tried everything he could think of to topple the Japanese giant. He pushed and pulled, shoved and heaved against the enormous, power-packed bulk of Tsunami's heavy-set body but nothing seemed to work. And while it was a kick getting his hands on the man again and feeling the undeniable masculinity of his ample size and strength, Randy got so caught up trying to defeat his opponent that he really didn't have time to enjoy it.

For his part, Tsunami wore the forced, grudging smile of an indulgent champion while he went through the motions of fending off Randy's determined but totally ineffectual attack. He was relaxed, in complete control and patiently biding his time. It soon became apparent he was going to let the precocious gaijin work up a sweat, so he'd have something to tell the folks back home about, then slam-dunk the little fucker into oblivion. A nice, simple strategy. Too bad things didn't go according to plan.

It was one of those weird, beginner's luck kind of moves. In the midst of a last-ditch frontal assault, Randy somehow managed to plant a leg behind the sumotori and use it to trip the unsuspecting stud. Tsunami stumbled, lost his balance completely and with a surprised grunt landed flat on his back with Randy sprawled out on top of him.

There was a moment of stunned silence and then, amused and delighted by the outcome, the stablemaster and his fellow spectators erupted in wild whoops and hollers and swarmed around the two wrestlers. There were hearty congratulations for a dazed but happy Randy and a lot of good-natured ribbing for Tsunami, who could best be described as stoic. The celebration was short and sweet but it was clear that Randy had made a lasting impression and was going to enter the annals of sumo folk lore. Randy the Giant Killer, they were calling him!

It was only when the last back-slapping rikishi had left that Randy, still aglow from his victory, turned and saw the scowl on Tsunami's face. The man was grim. Real grim. "Oh-oh."

At that precise moment Kenzo's cellular phone rang. The tension mounted while Kenzo took the call and the two wrestlers were forced to cool their heels. When he hung up, Kenzo apologized profusely and said that Mr. Hashimoto needed him back at the office. "Don't worry, Randy, you still have the rest of the day off," were his parting words. Boy, did he look relieved to be getting out of there.

Alone together at last, Randy shrugged and gave a feeble, half-hearted smile. "It was a fluke," he mumbled.

The dark brown eyes never wavered, the voice was cold. "I demand a re-match."

Randy knew there was no way out. Fluke or no fluke, by losing to a mere gaijin Tsunami had lost face in front of his stablemates. Honor had to be restored. This was not going to be pretty. He took a deep breath and said, "Okay. Right here, right now."

With little visible emotion, Tsunami went over to the door and snapped the lock. He returned to the center of the room and ominously intoned, "I don't want to be disturbed."

Randy swallowed hard. "You're right. Some things are best done in private."

Tsunami's face twisted into a determined snarl. "Now you're going to find out just how big and strong I really am."

"Fuck, I hope so," replied Randy, with as much bravado as he could muster. Deep down, though, he was concerned and more than just a little worried. Tsunami had the size and strength to do some real damage. Worse, he had a lot of anger and humiliation to motivate him and no ropes or outside interference to hold him back. And while Randy wanted the big man, he also wanted to be in one piece when the dust settled.

Just as he feared, Randy was barely into his three-point stance when the vengeful sumotori exploded out of his crouch and slammed into him with the full force of his massive, muscular frame. Tsunami was as good as his nickname, colliding like a ten-ton tidal wave in a clean but nonetheless devastating hit clearly designed to soften up his opponent. It sure worked against the unsuspecting gaijin.

Randy had the wind knocked right out of him and a thousand stars burst in front of his eyes. He would have been thrown flat on his ass if Tsunami hadn't grabbed him by the arms and suddenly yanked him like a yo-yo back against the ample curve of his substantial, overhanging gut.

"What do you think of sumo now?" sneered Tsunami. With a laugh he forced Randy's face down into the crevice between his two huge, gorilla-like pecs and then roughly dragged it back and forth across the curved mounds of his chest. "You like that? You like your gaijin face rubbed against big Japanese pecs?"

He pushed Randy's mouth against a soft, rubbery nipple and barked, "Suck it! Suck my tit like you mean it. Yeah, that's it. Harder. Harder! Good boy! Now give me some teeth. Chew it, really chew it! Let me feel it! Chow down on those tits and give me something to remember! Yeahhh!"

It wasn't until both nipples were red and raw and pumped to incredible cow-teat proportions that Tsunami seemed satisfied. He picked Randy up again and pulled him in for a serious, bone-crushing bearhug.

"O-mi-god!" gasped Randy, as he felt the life being squeezed right out of him. A myriad of emotions and sensations swept over him as he fought against going under. Part of him was angry and wanted to deck the Japanese giant for what he was being put through. Restoring honor, not to mention getting repaid for the scene at the dungeon, was one thing but getting put through the grinder like this was quite another.

Still another part of him—a much larger part—was not only turned on by all the rough treatment but couldn't believe how excited he got by the combination of powerful, over-developed muscle and abundant, corpulent beef. It was wild, fucking wild. He wanted the man, wanted the big, strong, heavy-set man to punish, use and abuse him in the worst way possible because, fuck, he *liked* it!

Then something else kicked in. Randy knew Tsunami had to win this match eventually but, dammit, he was not a quitter and had his own honor to uphold. Hard aching cock or no hard aching cock, he was fucked if he was going to make it easy for the brute.

Filled with a new resolve, Randy shirked the passive role he'd been given and went on the attack. It took a bit of frantic bucking and shaking but he managed to slip out of Tsunami's tight, sweaty grasp and regain his feet. Then he quickly plowed into the big man with a series of hard shoulder blocks which managed to knock the wind out of the surprised sumotori and give him a chance to latch onto the two swollen nipples.

"You like titwork?" he snapped. "I'll give you titwork!" And with that Randy viciously twisted the two throbnobs and forced

Tsunami down to his knees. What came next was cruel and depraved but, deep down, Randy knew Tsunami was getting off on it. He also knew they both wanted more (not that titwork isn't a whole enjoyable trip unto itself) so, while still playing with Tsunami's tits he ordered, "Take off that fucking mawashi! Strip down and let's get that cock out in the open!"

Grimacing from the pain radiating from his chest, Tsunami fumbled with the folds of his mawashi. It took a while (Randy suspected Tsunami deliberately prolonged the tit workout) but at last the mawashi lay in a heap on the floor. Free of its restraints, Tsunami's hefty bull balls dropped low in their sac between his legs and his thick tube of cut manmeat sprang up and surged to its awesome, fully-engorged state.

Contrary to the rumor Kenzo had been so eager to pass along, Tsunami was not seven inches. No, he was closer to nine. Nine very long, very thick inches. Not only that but those nine very long, very thick inches were topped with a large, bulbous head the likes of which could choke a horse. It was a magnificent cock of epic proportions which caused Randy's own cock to do some surging of its own.

Major error in judgment, getting distracted like that. Tsunami's hands shot out, grabbed Randy behind the ankles and yanked the legs right out from under him. Even more surprising was how fast he managed to get on top of him, straddling him across the waist and pinning his wrists against the floor. Ignoring the frantic, quite useless attempts at escape, he leaned down close to Randy's contorted face and jeered, "Stupid mistake, little man. What's the matter, you act like you never seen a big Asian dick before. You forget Saturday night already? Here, take a good look. Refresh memory."

Tsunami scooted up so that his "big Asian dick" hovered mere inches above Randy's head. He took hold of his cock and used it as a club to beat Randy about the face until he had Randy practically in tears from the pain, frustration and humiliation. "You like that? You like my big Asian dick in your face?" he kept taunting.

Getting to his feet, Tsunami hauled Randy to his knees and said, "Now you're going to take my big Asian dick down your skinny gaijin throat. Open up. Open up, I said! Good boy. Now, suck it. Suck my big dick and make me a happy man!"

He started off angry and resentful (who needs all the macho attitude shit, he griped) but the more Randy got into blowing the big hunk of manmeat the more he had to concede the job was a real labor of lust. With Tsunami's gut pressing against the top of his head he hung onto the sumotori's heavy cum-filled bull balls and feverishly made a meal of the tasty meatus. He lapped at the huge cockhead, tickled the wide pisshole, stroked the thick throbbing shaft and deep-throated as much of the juicy megaprick as he could. Okay, fuck, he loved it. Loved every fucking inch of it!

What began as begrudging restitution turned into an all-out frenzy of depraved dick worship. If there was one thing Randy was good at it was sucking cock. Even a cock as big as Tsunami's. He worked it like crazy and in no time had the sweaty sumotori eating out of the palm of his hand. So to speak.

"Yes. Oh fuck, yes," Tsunami exclaimed. "That's it. Oh fuck, yes, that feels good. Suck that cock. Suck it. Oh! Ohhh! Oh fuck, yes!" He revved wildly out of control and with little or no consideration yanked Randy to his feet, ripped his shorts off, spun him around and bent him over so that he had clear access to the bare gaijin bubblebutt.

"Hey!" protested Randy. He made a concerted effort to protect his backside but Tsunami was too strong for him. He heard the saliva get hucked into his crack and seconds later felt the spit being massaged into his tight little hole with the aid of a thick middle finger. He struggled again (more out of a sense of obligation) but stopped dead in his tracks when yet another thick digit went up his hole. "O-mi-god!" he groaned, surrendering to the wonderful sphincter stretching sensations.

But all too soon the fingers were pulled out and the forbidding, cum-dripping cockhead pressed against the tiny portal. "This is where you roll over and get fucked by a zip code," hissed Tsunami. And then, in one hard savage thrust, he rammed his mighty piledriver right to the hilt up Randy's quivering shitchute.

Randy threw back his head, arched his spine, let out a groan to wake the dead and almost passed out, the pain was so intense. He tried wriggling free but Tsunami held him tight around the waist and kept him impaled on his Japanese joystick. It was almost too much, even for an accommodating hole like Randy's. He kept repeating "Omigod! Omigod! Ooommiiigoooddd!" over and over again like it was some mantra that could channel the pain away.

Tsunami was a hard-core, heavy duty, kamikaze kind of butt-fucker. Gentle he was not. Probably wants to teach the gaijin a lesson, figured Randy. Then, too, there's a hell of a lot of weight being thrown around back there and maybe the big guy just doesn't realize his own size and strength, he reasoned. Yeah, right. Whatever, Randy got plowed hard and deep with each unrelenting stroke. Bam! Bam! Bam!

The mantra must have done some good, though, because it wasn't all that long before Randy not only accepted the pleasure/pain radiating from his ass but met Tsunami's bestial buttfucking rhythm with some enthusiastic back and forth butt action of his own. He wasn't usually on the receiving end but there was just something about the way Tsunami plowed him that made his cock rock-hard and had him moaning and groaning and begging for more.

He got into it so much that when a tired and sweaty Tsunami indicated he wanted to take a momentary breather Randy almost went crazy. The sumotori was still hard but the heat and humidity, his immense bulk and the fact that he'd already put in a long morning of practice conspired against him. Randy, however, was way too far along to quit now. Anxious to get what he wanted, he made the exhausted wrestler lie face up on the floor and squatted down on the erect cock. Once securely stuffed into his hungry hole he commenced to bouncing up and down on it like some little kid on an amusement park ride. In no time his buttfucking rhythm was back up to speed and his new mantra was a rapid-fire "Oh yeah! Oh yeah! Oh yeah!"

The fuck was a real kick and a half but, while he couldn't explain it, what Randy found really mind-blowing was getting turned on by someone who was just so . . . well, fat. No other word for it. Sure the guy had the build of a powerlifter but it couldn't be denied that he also carried a hell of a lot of excess chub. He, Randy Wilson, a confirmed card-carrying muscle queen (god, he hated that term) had been turned on by chub!

All Randy could think of while riding that major piece of meat was how much he loved, really loved, running his hands over the broad expanse of Tsunami's smooth, full belly. He loved how the hot, sweaty mound of Tsunami's sagging gut rolled and swayed and jiggled under him, how it almost seemed to move with a life of its own. Fuck, he wanted it. Wanted to hold it, caress it, knead it, press it, lose himself in it, be smothered by it. All of it! Every big, beautiful fantastic pound of it!

In his frenzied butt-induced excitement Randy reached up, latched onto Tsunami's swollen, tender nipples and used the engorged nubs for leverage in a bid to further intensify the rear-end action. Boom! That was the detonator. A couple of seconds into the tit-cock combo and Tsunami's super-charged cum-filled balls couldn't take it any longer.

Tsunami let out a loud roar, mashed Randy down on his hard throbbing dick and held him there while his overheated fuckpole exploded in a major bone-jarring orgasm. Feeling the gusher of warm, creamy cum filling his insides was all the trigger Randy needed for a raucous, super-intense orgasm of his own. Back went his head in a silent scream and then, without so much as a finger on his throbbing cock, he shot a heavy load all over Tsunami's heaving upper body. Yeah, creamed him good. By the time he was finished and his balls hung low and empty, big thick gobs of pearly jizz lay sparkling all over Tsunami's arms, shoulders, pecs and gut. Even the man's face got hit.

Spent, Randy collapsed onto Tsunami's inviting, hot and humpy cum-slicked torso. Big muscular arms wrapped around him in a secure, protective embrace, squeezing him tighter still against the massive, blubbery belly, provided the icing on the cake. Now he was truly happy. He'd not only had a fantastic fuck but had successfully fulfilled his obligations to the handsome Japanese hunk. What more could any gaijin want?

It wasn't until Tsunami's softening dick slid out of Randy's tingling, tender ass that the silence in the room was finally broken. "You are a most worthy opponent, Randy-san. I would be honored if we could have another match someday," said the sumotori.

"Someday soon, real soon," replied Randy.

"Tonight? My place?"

"You're on, big guy."

"Excellent. Most excellent. Oh, and bring your ropes."

Tool Pusher

AN OIL DERRICK is like a cock looking for a blowjob. It's the upright framework for equipment which sends a drill bit and thousands of feet of pipe deep into solid rock in an attempt to reach the pools of black cum buried in the balls of the earth. Most times, dick-all happens. But with a good lead hand and a bit of luck, the rig hits paydirt, erupts in a gooey mechanical orgasm and makes everyone very, very happy.

One particular derrick stood 142 feet straight up in the hot summer sky, the pivot for a camp stuck in the middle of west Texas scrubland. Camp Blue-2 was run by a mean son of a bitch tool pusher named Hank. His nickname was "The Shank" and it only took a glance in the showers to figure out why. Soft, his cock was about the size of a beer can. Erect, it was three inches in diameter and eleven long inches of mean-looking, uncut meat.

Everyone in the oilpatch knew the measurements because last winter Joe Caputo put his money where his mouth was and bet Hank that he had the bigger cock. Hank just hauled out his meat right there in the bunkhouse and beat it to a standing position. It was duly measured to make sure everything was fair and square but everyone could see Joe didn't stand a chance. Caputo lost a thousand bucks that night and left with his puny pecker between his legs.

Hank's 5′10″ frame was packed with 185 pounds of pure, hard muscle, the kind made by twenty-five years of ball-busting work. He looked like a cross between a fireplug and a small bear, especially with the thick, black hair that covered his body. The only concession to his 40 years was the thinning hair on his head—but it wasn't something a smart man mentioned.

Hank reached into his coveralls and idly scratched his left tit. In hot weather he never wore anything under the rough fabric and kept the zipper open down to his navel. He was sweating like a stuck pig that day, so the wet coveralls clung to every muscle, rode high up his crack, and hugged the thick meat stuffed down the right pant leg.

In front of him stood a new addition to the crew. Hank didn't usually like greenhorn roughnecks—they were either stupid, slow or weak—but this one looked different and he hoped the guy would be the exception. Especially since his cock had started twitching, which was always a good sign.

Ken was only 21 but, at 6′2″, 215 pounds, he was built like a brick shithouse. Blond, blue-eyed and tanned a golden brown, he had lifted weights from the time he was twelve. And it showed. In fact, he loved bodybuilding so much that he was only truly happy when pumping heavy iron surrounded by big muscle studs doing the same.

"I see you slack-assing just once, and you'll get the shit kicked out of you!" barked Hank. "Roughnecking is a man's job and needs all the muscle you got."

"I got muscle," replied Ken, stating the obvious. What gives? This guy was reaming him out and he was barely off the truck. "I lift weights, sir."

Hank liked the way that "sir" came out and his cock gave another twitch. His balls tightened and his hand went down to give them a tug. "Lifting barbells ain't worth diddly-squat compared to wrestling oilfield iron, asshole!"

Ken's eyes dropped to the open V of the coveralls and checked out the thick pecs and defined abdominals. He never thought he'd see such hard-packed, chiseled muscle outside a gym. Then he saw the outline of Hank's dick. "Holy shit!"

"What the fuck are you staring at, asshole?"

Deciding to shoot the works, Ken looked Hank right in the eye and replied, "You're in good shape, sir."

"You're fucking right I am. And you'll find just what kind of shape I'm in if I don't see you busting your ass all the time you're supposed to be working. Now, get the hell out of my sight. The cook'll show you where to stow your gear, then get your ass up to that derrick. *Move!*"

Hank scowled as Ken scooped up his gear and ran across the open camp to the cookhouse but, in truth, he was admiring the muscular young body. "The kid's got a damn good basket, too. And that ass looks like it was made for plowing."

Horny as hell now, Hank increased the pressure around the derrick and made the crew hustle to keep pace with him. By mid-day, everyone had the rhythm down pat and the hole sunk deeper and deeper towards the earth's core. Hard, fast and smooth—just the way Hank liked to see his rig operate.

Never too busy to look, Ken lusted after the humpy tool pusher with a passion. Since lunch he'd been working with a raging, rock-hard dick, imagining what it would be like to run his hand through all that chest hair and chow down on those mile-high tits. He couldn't wait to hit the showers, just to see if that bulge at Hank's crotch was for real.

For his part, Hank kept a careful eye on Ken. He was pleased to see that, while the kid did make the usual greenhorn mistakes, he made up for them with strength, agility and a certain driller-sense.

And, shit, what a body! Stripped to the waist, covered head to boot in grease and mud like he was, the hunky kid with the major muscles looked damn fucking impressive. No, more than impressive. With rivulets of sweat streaming down his awesome, jaw-dropping torso into the waistband of his soaked, skin-tight pants, he was definitely the ultimate in overt, in-your-face masculinity! It was all Hank could do not to break him in right then and there!

A couple of hours later a shout went up from the deck and Hank rushed out of the doghouse to see what was going on. Ken was sprawled on his ass with a stunned look on his face while the crew nervously gathered around offering advice.

"Okay, everyone else back to work!" barked Hank. He stood over Ken and snapped, "What the fuck happened to you?"

"I'm alright," mumbled Ken. He tried getting up but Hank's size 10 met him in the stomach and forced him back down.

Hank's boot dug deeper into Ken's stomach. "I asked you what happened, asshole!"

Sheepishly, Ken replied, "I leaned in too close to the kelly and got tapped on the head. I was wearing my hard-hat, so nothing happened."

The mud-stained boot slid down the six-pack abs, over the low-slung belt, and came to rest on the thick slab of meat. As if putting out a cigar, Hank ground his heel on the hard cock and asked, "Are you sure, asshole? I don't like filling out accident reports."

Contracting inward, Ken suddenly grabbed the boot and

mashed it harder into his balls as a powerful, all-encompassing orgasm pummelled his big, beefy body. Wad after wad of creamy spunk exploded from the mouth of his cock like rapid-fire artillery shells and coated the inside of his pants with sticky sperm. It took a while for the spasms to subside but, when they did, for the first time since arriving in camp Ken's dick went soft and the ache in his balls was gone.

"I guess that means you're alright," smirked Hank.

Smiling, Ken finally gasped out, "Thank you, sir."

Hank took one last look at the giant of a man sprawled beneath him and barked, "Back to work, asshole!" For good measure, he gave a short, vicious kick to Ken's tender groin.

Ken rolled on his side, moaning and clutching his nuts. "Thank you, sir." He took a deep breath and hurried to his job.

Hank ducked back into the doghouse, zipping up his coveralls so the crew couldn't see his raging boner. It hurt so much he finally had to stand in a corner and savagely beat off. With his free hand, he alternated between twisting his sore bull-nuts and mashing his tortured, bloated tits. It was only a matter of seconds before his cum spattered against the metal walls of the doghouse and slid in big, gooey gobs down to the floor.

Hank tried keeping busy in the doghouse for the rest of the afternoon, hoping to take his mind off the stud working outside, but his rod just wouldn't go down. Finally, he could take it no longer and called out to Ken, ordering him to follow. "I need help checking some drill pipe."

Like an obedient pup, Ken tailed Hank down off the substructure and along the tall pipe racks until they were hidden from the rig. Alone with Hank at last, he kept praying Hank was going to do more than just inspect pipe.

Hank stopped abruptly, zipped down his coveralls and pulled out his hard meat. "Gotta take a piss."

Ken's eyes widened on the cock. Holy fuckin' geezus! He'd never seen anything like that monster before. It looked downright inhuman and, for the first time, apprehension gnawed at his gut. What was he letting himself in for? "Maybe I better get back to the rig," he mumbled, taking a step back.

"Stay right where you are," snapped Hank. He took a step and without warning grabbed both of Ken's big nipples and twisted, hard.

His mouth open in a silent scream, Ken threw back his head and dropped to his knees. His broad chest heaved as waves of excruciating, delirious pain radiated through his body and collected in his cock, threatening to blow it to smithereens.

Again, Hank twisted the puckered spots, rolling them between his strong, callused fingers until Ken couldn't stand the punishment any longer and had to cry out.

Tits blazing atop a pounding chest, Ken was going crazy when Hank suddenly plugged his open mouth with his mean eleven inches and snarled, "Suck it good, asshole."

Ken tried, really tried, to make Hank proud of him but he slowly realized he couldn't do the monster club justice. It was just too much for him! He'd never even seen a cock that size before, let alone go down on one.

Disgusted by Ken's rather pathetic effort, Hank grabbed the kid's tits and hauled him to his feet. "That's the worst fucking blowjob I've ever had, asshole! Fuck, I gotta do everything around here. Drop those pants."

Scrambling to obey, Ken quickly pushed his Levis down to his ankles and stood at attention. Since he never wore shorts, his erect dick was out in the open and ready for action. A lattice-work of purple veins throbbed as they rushed blood up the bloated prong to the large, cut head while pre-cum dribbled down the shaft and dripped off the pendulous sac hanging low between his thighs.

Hank nodded in grudging admiration. The kid was not only built solid, but he had an impressive piece of equipment to match. He had guessed right about it being eight inches. Rolling the left ball between his thumb and forefinger, he couldn't help but smile when Ken winced at the pressure. "Okay, now take a lesson from the master!"

Dropping to his knees, Hank took the eight inch rod into his mouth right up to the balls and, like a heavy-duty vacuum cleaner, began sucking. He reached around and grabbed onto Ken's twin cheeks for support, sticking the middle finger of his right hand into the rosebud for good luck. Yup, he knew exactly what he was doing.

Ken quickly went out of his mind as Hank stepped up the assault on his fuckpole. He tried his damnedest to keep from detonating, but almost lost it when Hank released his cock and popped both balls into his mouth for a good chewing. The only thing that saved him was twisting his own nipples so hard he practically pulled them off his chest.

Hank's snake-like tongue darted along the kid's shaft, tickling the pisshole and tracing the path of each and every vein down to the sperm-laden scrotum. He mauled that cock like a hungry dog cleans a bone until, suddenly, Hank felt the cock quiver, the quick contraction and then . . . *bam!* The first wad hit deep against the roof of his mouth.

Then again. And again! As fast as the thick gobs of jism shot out, they disappeared down Hank's parched throat. He couldn't get enough of the white ambrosia.

The last of the juice swallowed, Hank stood and grabbed his throbbing cock, giving the thick shank a couple of slow, drawn-out strokes. "Turn around and bend over," he growled.

Horror-struck, Ken's 215 muscular-pounds actually started shaking. "Please, sir! I ain't never been butt-fucked with anything that—"

"Shut up, asshole! I never repeat an order twice!" Hank held out his cupped hand. "Spit good and hard, 'cause that's all the lube you're going to get.

"Now, bend over and grab your ankles!" Hank added a gob of his own spit to what Ken provided and lovingly smeared it along the length of his meat, which surged in anticipation of the fun before it. He worked up another gob and spit into Ken's hairless crack, guiding the spit into the tight, browny-pink butthole with his middle finger.

"You better loosen up, kid, or this baby's going to split your ass wide open!" The kid's whimpering only got Hank hornier. Fuck, he never wanted someone's ass as bad as he wanted this one.

Carefully, even gently, Hank worked the head of his cock past the tight ring of muscle. Grinding his hips real slow-like, he inched his dick into the hot, steamy tunnel and let Ken get used to it. He couldn't help smiling: it'd be a long time before Ken forgot this fuck.

Halfway in, Hank felt Ken's sphincter relax. The kid was beginning to enjoy himself. Good. Okay, enough of this pissing around, he thought, as he placed his arms firmly around Ken's waist. "This is where we separate the men from the boys."

With one animal thrust, Hank buried his tool to the hilt up Ken's shitchute. If it weren't for the noise of the camp's motors, Ken's agonized groan would have brought the whole crew running. He thrashed around for a while, but Hank held him firm and the kid didn't go anywhere.

Slipping off the top of his coveralls for more freedom, Hank got down to the serious business at hand. With the sweat pouring off him, he looked up and soaked in the last rays of west Texas sun as the instinctive, almost mechanical rhythm of his humping slowly raised the pressure in his cock. His fucking was like the way he ran his rig: work fast and always go deep using the best equipment available. And he knew his cock was the best drill pipe around for boring ass.

Faster and faster Hank went. Each time, he just about pulled right out before slamming all eleven inches back into his sheath. He loved the sensation of a thousand needles jabbing his sac each time his balls got mashed between him and the bedrock of Ken's cheeks. It drove him mental with the added pain and torment. Drilling was more than a profession with Hank. It was his whole life, his reason for being and, *damn*, he was good at it!

Shit, he barely felt it in time, he was so into it! The skin pulled back tight along his cock and the explosion went off in his balls as an invisible hand ferociously grabbed and twisted his nuts.

Throwing his head back as he arched his spine and proudly offered his chest skyward, Hank plunged in and blasted his first wad deep, real deep into Ken's writhing gut.

Another stab from his diamond-hard cock and more spunk was planted. His body quaked as the third and fourth shots of hot, sticky crude rocketed forth. It was about that time when Ken joined him in an orgasm of his own. Yeah, the kid was fucking hot, alright.

Breathing a deep sigh of relief when he finished, Hank pumped a few more times before finally pulling out. "You're a good fuck, asshole," he said, running his hand tenderly over the kid's smooth, muscular butt.

Ken winced at Hank's sudden withdrawal, certain that his ass had been ripped to shreds by the tool pusher's size and rough treatment. In the back of his mind, though, he was also wondering when he could get Hank's meat up his hungry hole again.

Pulling on his coveralls and stuffing his equipment back behind the zipper, Hank looked over at the humpy young stud and chuckled, "You and me are going to get along just fine."

Just then one of the roughnecks appeared at the other end of the pipe rack and shouted, "Bin looking for you all over the place, Hank. We struck oil! It's a gusher!"

Squeezing his cock, Hank laughed. "You're fuckin' telling me! Come on, asshole, pull up your pants. We got a well to cap."

AIDS RISK REDUCTION GUIDELINES FOR HEALTHIER SEX

As given by Bay Area Physicians for Human Rights

NO RISK: *Most of these activities involve only skin-to-skin contact, thereby avoiding exposure to blood, semen, and vaginal secretions. This assumes there are no breaks in the skin.* **1) Social kissing** (dry). **2) Body massage, hugging. 3) Body to body rubbing** (frottage). **4) Light S&M** (without bruising or bleeding). **5) Using one's own sex toys. 6) Mutual masturbation** (male or external female). Care should be taken to avoid exposing the partners to ejaculate or vaginal secretions. Seminal, vaginal and salivary fluids should not be used as lubricants.

LOW RISK: *In these activities small amounts of certain body fluids might be exchanged, or the protective barrier might break causing some risk.* **1) Anal or vaginal intercourse with condom.** Studies have shown that HIV does not penetrate the condom in simulated intercourse. Risk is incurred if the condom breaks or if semen spills into the rectum or vagina. The risk is further reduced if one withdraws before climax. **2) Fellatio interruptus** (sucking, stopping before climax). Pre-ejaculate fluid may contain HIV. Saliva or other natural protective barriers in the mouth may inactivate virus in pre-ejaculate fluid. Saliva may contain HIV in low concentration. The insertive partner should warn the receptive partner before climax to prevent exposure to a large volume of semen. If mouth or genital sores are present, risk is increased. Likewise, action which causes mouth or genital injury will increase risk. **3) Fellatio with condom** (sucking with condom) Since HIV cannot penetrate an intact condom, risk in this practice is very low unless breakage occurs. **4) Mouth-to-mouth kissing** (French kissing, wet kissing) Studies have shown that HIV is present in saliva in such low concentration that salivary exchange is unlikely to transmit the virus. Risk is increased if sores in the mouth or bleeding gums are present. **5) Oral-vaginal or oral-anal contact with protective barrier.** e.g. a latex dam, obtainable through a local dental supply house, may be used. Do not reuse latex barrier, because sides of the barrier may be reversed inadvertently. **6) Manual anal contact with glove** (manual anal (fisting) or manual vaginal (internal) contact with glove). If the glove does not break, virus transmission should not occur. However, significant trauma can still be inflicted on the rectal tissues leading to other medical problems, such as hemorrhage or bowel perforation. **7) Manual vaginal contact with glove** (internal). See above.

MODERATE RISK: *These activities involve tissue trauma and/or exchange of body fluids which may transmit HIV or other sexually transmitted disease.* **1) Fellatio** (sucking to climax). Semen may contain high concentrations of HIV and if absorbed through open sores in the mouth or digestive tract could pose risk. **2) Oral-anal contact** (rimming). HIV may be contained in blood-contaminated feces or in the anal rectal lining. This practice also poses high risk of transmission of parasites and other gastrointestinal infections. **3) Cunnilingus** (oral-vaginal contact). Vaginal secretions and menstrual blood have been shown to harbor HIV, thereby causing risk to the oral partner if open lesions are present in the mouth or digestive tract. **4) Manual rectal contact** (fisting). Studies have indicated a direct association between fisting and HIV infection for both partners. This association may be due to concurrent use of recreational drugs, bleeding, pre-fisting semen exposure, or anal intercourse with ejaculation. **5) Sharing sex toys. 6) Ingestion of urine.** HIV has not been shown to be transmitted via urine; however, other immunosuppressive agents or infections may be transmitted in this manner.

HIGH RISK: *These activities have been shown to transmit HIV.* **1) Receptive anal intercourse without condom.** All studies imply that this activity carries the highest risk of transmitting HIV. The rectal lining is thinner than that of the vagina or the mouth thereby permitting ready absorption of the virus from semen or pre-ejaculate fluid to the blood stream. One laboratory study suggests that the virus may enter by direct contact with rectal lining cells without any bleeding. **2) Insertive anal intercourse without condom.** Studies suggest that men who participate only in this activity are at less risk of being infected than their partners who are rectally receptive; however the risk is still significant. It carries high risk of infection by other sexually transmitted diseases. **3) Vaginal intercourse without condom.**